THONGOR AT THE END OF TIME

For seven nights Mardanax, the masked magician, has readied himself for his revenge on Thongor. The crypts and catacombs beneath the palace have witnessed many grim and terrible scenes of torment and punishment, but none so awful as the black rites wherewith the Black Druid prepares himself for the hour of his triumph. Each dawn the rushing waters of the Twin Rivers bear out to sea the obscenely mutilated corpses of certain slaves from whose skin the telltale ownership mark has been removed—pitiful cadavers whose life-force, brutally torn from agonized flesh, has been offered up in sacrifice to the Triple Lord of Chaos.

NOW MARDANAX STRIKES—AND THONGOR FALLS LIFELESS!

Other Books
by
Lin Carter

Thongor Against The Gods
Thongor in The City of Magicians

Published by
WARNER BOOKS

THONGOR
at the
END OF TIME

by Lin Carter

WARNER BOOKS

A Warner Communications Company

THONGOR AT THE END OF TIME
is dedicated to
John Jakes, Roy Krenkel, *and* Roy Langbord
Kojans of the Empire

WARNER BOOKS EDITION

Copyright © 1968 by Paperback Library, Inc.

ISBN: 0-446-94332-0

Warner Books, Inc., 75 Rockefeller Plaza, New York, N.Y. 10019

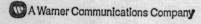 A Warner Communications Company

Printed in the United States of America

First Printing: October, 1968

Reissued: December, 1979

10 9 8 7 6 5 4 3 2

Table of Contents

THE FIRST BOOK: THE MASKED MAGICIAN

1.	The Black Robed One	10
2.	At the Altar of the Nineteen Gods	17
3.	The Secret Council	23
4.	The Flying Man	28

THE SECOND BOOK: THONGOR IN THE LAND OF SHADOWS

5.	The Dweller on the Threshold	36
6.	The Sword in the Jewel	43
7.	The Road of Millions of Years	49
8.	River of Fire, Wall of Ice	54

THE THIRD BOOK: SLAVES OF THE PIRATE EMPIRE

9.	Above the Clouds	61
10.	In the Dragons' Grip	68
11.	Barim Redbeard	74
12.	A Knife in the Back	82

THE FOURTH BOOK: THONGOR AMONG THE GODS

13.	Lord of Starry Wisdom	91
14.	Behind the Stars	97
15.	The Lord of the Three Truths	102
16.	A Billion Tomorrows	107

THE FIFTH BOOK: AT SWORD'S POINT

17.	In the Pirate City	116
18.	Black Catacombs	124
19.	Race Against Time	131
20.	Out of the Shadows!	138

APPENDIX: The Source of the Lemurian Mythos 150

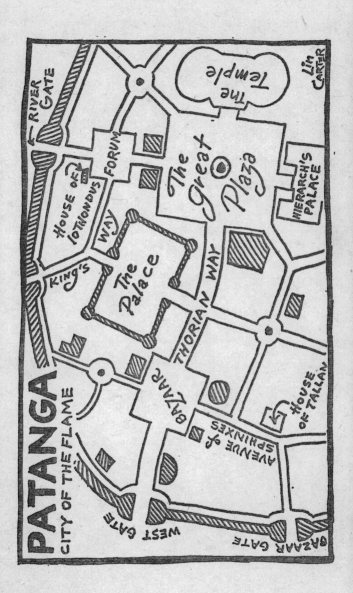

PATANGA
CITY OF THE FLAME

River Gate
House of Iothondus
Forum Way
King's Way
The Palace
Thorian Way
The Great Plaza
The Temple
Hierarch's Palace
House of Tallan
Bazaar
Avenue of Sphinxes
West Gate
Bazaar Gate

Lin Carter

The First Book

THE MASKED MAGICIAN

"... Greatness came upon Patanga the City of the Flame in the days after Zaar of the Magicians was whelmed and trodden down in ruin beneath the Unknown Sea; and in the fullness of time six proud cities came to stand under the black-and-golden banners of Thongor the Mighty, and lo! the gods were pleased. But that grim and unappeasable Fate that triumphs even over the gods and is not swayed by the splendor and power of kings, smote the Warrior of the West with the strangest of dooms, and the jaws of Death gaped wide to engulf his unconquerable spirit. . . ."

—*The Lemurian Chronicles*
Book Five, Ch. i.

Chapter 1: THE BLACK-ROBED ONE

> The gods inscrutable and old
> With vision that can scan the past
> And know what dim tomorrows hold,
> Bring Thongor down to death at last. . . .

> —*Thongor's Saga*, Stave XVIII

Thongor the Mighty clutched at his throat. He swayed, staggering, as he stood there at the high altar in the great temple of his royal city of Patanga. His breast heaved, his lungs labored, panting for air. With one hand he tore away the rich embroidered robes of state, baring his panting chest whereon a small amulet of green paste dangled on a thong about his corded throat. He fought against the numbness that spread like icy venom through his veins—strove to beat back the swirling crimson mists that fogged his vision. As the light thickened about him, he could see dimly through the gathering shadows the astonished faces of his lords and captains, courtiers and nobles—among them, the white face of his lovely mate, Sumia, and the frightened features of his young son, Prince Thar. Noon sun struck splendidly through the thronged temple where his entourage was gathered to watch the Lord of the West conduct the spring offering to the gods.

Instead, they saw a different kind of offering. . . .

Then his strength failed him, and he fell sprawling down the marble steps to lie like a dead thing at the base of the altar. Shouts rang out and women shrieked in the terror and confusion. Old Lord Mael, one of the chief peers and advisors of Thongor, was standing to the forefront of the crowd and was thus the first to reach the side of the fallen king. He laid his ear against the motionless chest of the

10

barbarian, then examined the body with shaking hands. When he lifted his face to Sumia Sarkaja, his bluff and hearty visage was grimly pale, shadowed with loss.

The young queen stood with her slim arms about the prince her son, comforting the frightened boy. She did not need Mael's hesitant words to know that her savage and kingly mate was dead.

But this is not the beginning of the tale. For that, we must turn back the pages of the Book of Time to a moment some fifteen days before these events came to pass. The place is the great West Gate of Patanga. It is the hour after dawn. For here the mighty tale of Thongor's most awesome and fantastic adventure truly begins . . .

It was early one morning in the spring of the Year of the Kingdoms of Man 7017. Charn Thovis, the young Otar of the Black Dragons who had saved the life of Thongor three years before during the ambush at the Hills of the Thunder-Crystals, had risen with dawn as was his wont. Thongor had rewarded his courage with the captaincy of a hundred warriors and ennobled him as a *kojan* of the empire. Thus he resided in the Palace of a Hundred Sarks whose towering mass of masonry rose on the Thorian Way, that mighty avenue that ran from the Great Plaza at the center of the gorgeous metropolis to the soaring bastions of the West Gate. Thither he strolled this morning as the gold sun of ancient Lemuria rose above the edges of the world and flooded all the land with light.

He was a tall, lithe-limbed young warrior, this Charn Thovis, his tanned and lean and powerful body half-bared in the Lemurian harness of black leathern straps, the coveted dragon emblem blazoned on his accouterments and swordhilt. He had a strong-jawed, clean-shaven face with clear gray eyes and straight black hair worn close-cropped. His boot heels rang on the stone pave as he strode through the streets. A vast black cloak belled from his broad shoulders and sunlight glittered on the gems he wore at armlet, girdle and hilt.

The towering gates of Patanga were swung asunder with

11

dawn, for the mighty Spring Rites were near and already lumbering zamphs dragged massive wains laden with grain and fruit and produce from the outlying farms to market in the famed bazaar of the City of the Flame. Through the gates of the walled city streamed a motley horde. Farmers and peasants on their way to market. A wandering bard; a juggler or two. Here rode a cloaked warrior astride a lean, swift-pacing kroter, whose reptilian scales caught the morning sun and glittered. There the veiled palanquin of some lord or ambassador to the court of the mighty Lord of the West swung on the broad shoulders of Rmoahal slaves with gems in their ears.

And here and there among the others strode young men in war-harness, with swords at their sides or bows and quivers strapped across their shoulders—youths gray with road dust, weary and athirst, come hither from this or that of the Nine Cities of the West. From Zangabal or Pelorm or Shembis they came, from Tsargol and Cadorna and Thurdis the Dragon City, drawn to Great Patanga by the magic of Thongor's name and the legend of his mighty deeds. And Charn Thovis smiled to see them, for not too many years ago he had been one of their number, a youthful *chanthar* or warrior from distant Vozashpa to the East, scion of an ancient family of honorable descent now fallen on lean times. Hither had he come across half a world, to break with the past and pledge his sword to the great hero-king of the age, Thongor of Valkarth, Lord of the Six Cities.

Well, the lads would find their place among the legions of Imperial Patanga, either in the Host or perchance, if fortune favored them, among the Patangan Archers or the newly formed Air Guard, whose sparkling and silvery flying boats circled tirelessly in the fresh morning sky above the mighty city; or even in that most honored of all regiments, the Black Dragons, who were vowed to defend the life and body of their lord the Sarkon, his bride the Sarkaja, and the young Jasark their son. Room there was in the mailed legions of the City of the Flame, for although Thongor had wrought mightily in the nine years since he had risen to the throne beside the woman he loved, and

12

though four cities of his foes had fallen before him in war, and the empire had grown vast and strong and without peer in all the continent of old Lemuria, still jealous and powerful foes eyed Patanga and her glory with covetous eyes and plotted to bring her black-and-golden banners down into the dust.

Busied with these thoughts, Charn Thovis did not notice one unobtrusive limping figure who entered the city gates on the heels of a clattering troop of spearmen mounted on great war-zamphs. He was bent and slow-footed as if old, supporting his weight by leaning on a tall staff. His lean body was wrapped in tattered and dusty robes of shabby black cloth, and a torn hood was drawn close about his bowed head as if to keep the morning sunlight from his face.

The man in black, however, noticed the young warrior as he stood watching the passing throng, and came limping over to where he stood beside a pylon whereon stone glyphs listed the long-gone triumphs of King Numidon who had reigned of old when Patanga was young. The warrior turned to survey the shuffling robed figure as it came near. From the condition of the ragged garments, much soiled with road dust and wear, he surmised the old fellow to be a beggar.

"I am sorry, old man, I came out without my purse this morning," Charn Thovis said with a frank smile. "However, you will find charity for all at the palace gates where the city's poor are fed. . . ."

The hooded man shook his head slightly and spoke in a husky voice scarcely louder than a whisper.

"An old man's thanks to you, Highborn, but it is not your gold I ask, but your assistance. I seek the house of the Baron of Tallan, if you could direct me to it."

"Indeed? Well, nothing simpler! This avenue is the great Thorian Way. Follow it to the Bazaar Square and take the Avenue of Sphinxes which goes south from the square into the Merchant's Quarter; you will find the house you seek at the place where the avenue branches in twain, one branch going west to the Bazaar Gate and the other south through the quarter."

13

The old beggar bowed his thanks and shuffled off, soon to be lost amidst the throng. Charn Thovis stared after him thoughtfully.

"Now by Karchonda, God of Warriors!" he said aloud, "that is truly an odd thing—"

"What is an odd thing, Charn Thovis?" a deep booming voice broke into his thoughts inquiringly. The young warrior turned to see the stalwart figure of a towering Rmoahal warrior in resplendent jeweled harness smiling down at him from his lofty height.

"*Belarba,* Shangoth," he welcomed the newcomer with the familiar Lemurian word of greeting. "You are early risen!"

"No more so than yourself." Shangoth grinned. The mighty Rmoahal, eight feet tall, bald as an egg, and indigo-blue of skin, was one of the great Nomad warriors of the remotest East, prince of the Jegga Horde whom Thongor had befriended eight years ago when adventuring on the Great Plains. Shangoth and several warriors of his princely retinue had accompanied the great Valkarthan back to Patanga to become members of his personal guard, and the brave Rmoahal with his simple barbaric dignity and deep-felt loyalty to the Lord of the West had swiftly made friends among Thongor's chief nobles and guardsmen despite his strange appearance and amazing height. Shangoth repeated his query. "When I came up you were muttering something about an odd thing. What was it?"

Charn Thovis rubbed his jaw thoughtfully. "Oh, nothing, really. An old beggar just entered the gates as I was standing here. He inquired directions to the House of Tallan, which is somewhat puzzling. . . ."

"Why is that puzzling?" Shangoth asked patiently.

"No particular reason, it's just—well, you perhaps do not know the Baron of Tallan, he rarely comes to Court for he is not very welcome there. His name is Dalendus Vool, a greasy toad of a man, noble in nothing save the title he inherited by accident of birth. He is a member of the Old Nobility, and somehow managed to remain in good odor when Lord Thongor liberated the City of the Flame from the grasp of the Fire Druids. The Sarkon exiled most of the

14

Old Nobility who had aided the cruel tyranny of the Druids, but there was no evidence against Dalendus Vool except an unsavory reputation. Anyway, I am puzzled that a beggar should seek out the House of Tallan, for I have never heard that Dalendus Vool was known for his charity—quite the opposite, I should have thought!"

Shangoth shrugged and laughed. "Well, if that is all you have to take up your time, vague suspicions of that nature, come—join me. Let us return to the palace. The day is young and we still have time aplenty for a brief workout with broadswords in the courtyard before the morning meal. Come—I will challenge you to a match!"

"And I will accept," Charn Thovis responded with a grin, "although I know from experience that to face you for a quarter-hour with broadswords means I shall be sore and aching for the rest of the day!"

They strode away chatting amiably, and it was not until many days later that Charn Thovis had cause to remember his first meeting with the black-robed beggar.

The Bent, hobbling figure in tattered and dusty robes limped and shuffled slowly along the Avenue of Sphinxes and reached by mid-morning the mansion of Dalendus Vool. It was a towering and palatial edifice whose ornate façade was rich with colored tiles whereon fantastic monsters capered amidst armorial bearings and geometrical designs.

The beggar made his slow and limping way to the rear of the mansion and entered through the kitchens. The delicious odors of cooking meat were thick in the smoky air and cooks bustled about decanting chilled wine and heaping trays of bright dewy fruit. Delicate pastries stood on a wooden table and meat pies were being drawn from steaming ovens by bare-chested apprentices—all this for one man, for as was well known, Dalendus Vool was a great gourmet who found his pleasure in the heavy-laden table and the well-filled winecup rather than in field of chase or in tourney or war.

So unobtrusive was the humble figure of the beggar and so quiet his entry into the kitchens that, for a few moments,

15

no one even noticed his presence. It was not until the chamberlain, a fat-cheeked and over-important little man, came bustling into the room to demand word of the progress of the meal that the beggar was noticed. He goggled at the calm figure and his face reddened with fury.

"Who let this tatterdemalion in from the gutters?" he squeaked. "You there! About your business and quickly, or I'll set the guard on you! If my lord were to know that street-beggars wander in and out of—of—" His voice wavered and died. His eyes goggled with astonishment and his red face paled swiftly.

Before his eyes the hunched figure straightened to its full height. Now the cold iron of aloof and kingly command radiated from the lean, black-robed form and eyes of lambent emerald flame blazed with cold malignant fires from the gaunt face whose features were shadowed and hidden by the close-drawn hood. Something in those weird flaming eyes—some unearthly power, some premonition of danger, chilled the very blood in the fat chamberlain's veins. The man in black surveyed him contemptuously from his lean height, taking in the pale-faced, quaking figure with a sneer of vicious humor. His voice, when he spoke, was an evil silken purr, ominous and chilling.

"Go to thy master, dog, and say that *his* master hath come. Aye, one he and all the world thinks dead and drowned beneath the cold waves of Takonda Chann the Unknown Sea these three long years, but who hath 'scaped the holocaust, eluding the wrath of the barbarian dog, Thongor, and who yet lives to see the dog of Valkarth cold and lifeless in his tomb! Go, fool, and summon my slave Dalendus Vool unto the presence of the Black Lord."

Terror was written plain to see in the chamberlain's goggling eyes and sweat-smeared brow and loose, working lips, but he had learned ere now from the kiss of a whip not to disturb the baron without full cause, so he summoned from deep within him enough courage to quaver a single question. "What . . . name?"

The emerald eyes flashed with cold witchfires as thin lips moved to pronounce the dreaded name of one long dead. *"Mardanax of Zaar!"*

16

Chapter 2:   AT THE ALTAR OF THE NINETEEN
GODS

> When great Zaar fell, one single man
> Escaped the floods while all the rest
> Went down to doom. 'Tis now his plan
> To wreak black vengeance on the West.
>
> —*Thongor's Saga,* Stave XVIII

Three years before these events took place, the air armada
of Patanga brought down to ultimate defeat Zaar the dead
City of Magicians in the culmination of a mighty war between the free men of the West and the age-old Black City
of the uttermost East. Armed with the new lightning guns
devised by the great Nephelos, Iothondus of Kathool, the
legions of Thongor wrought terrible destruction to the
stronghold of evil sorcery, and breached the giant sea wall
of black marble—loosing the titanic waves of Takonda
Chann the Unknown Sea, which whelmed and crushed the
Black City. Thus died the last of the Black Brotherhood
who had long sought to gain ascendancy by their weird
science and alien sorcery over the bright young cities of the
West.

And in that cataclysm died the last of the Nine Wizards,
those supreme and terrible masters of magic who had come
perilously close to bringing the Kingdoms of Man beneath
their iron tyranny. Made captive by superior force, dragged
as helpless slaves into the grim jaws of the dark gates of
Zaar, Thongor the Mighty and his friend Shangoth the
great Rmoahal warrior had burst their bonds and brought
crimson death to the Nine Lords of Zaar before the sky
fleets struck from the cloud-veiled heavens. The great

17

bronze war ax of the Nomad prince cut down Vual the Brain, Sarganeth of the Nuld, and Xoth the Skull. Thongor himself in a mighty duel slew the Red Prince, while the temple was collapsing under the assault of the flying ships of Patanga—burying under tons of masonry the corpse of Pytumathon, thus joined in death with Adamancus and Thalaba the Destroyer.

The world believed that Mardanax the Black Archdruid died in that holocaust. But in the howling chaos of the moment, while Thongor was battling against Maldruth the Scarlet, the Black Master of Zaar crept from his ebon throne and vanished through a secret door. Thence by obscure and hidden ways the masked magician fled his ancient city and escaped its terrible doom—but at a price. Shorn of his magical weapons and instruments, his powers weakened, lost or dispersed, alone and friendless in a hostile land where his great power was at last ended, Mardanax faced the grim task of making his way across half a continent filled with his foes. Somehow he had accomplished this mighty quest. The perils he surmounted, the dangers he eluded, the hazards he overcame could make a thrilling epic of adventure. But that tale shall go forever untold, for it is written not in *The Lemurian Chronicles*.

Now was he come at last into the very camp of his enemies. In secret and alone he had made his way up the great gulf, that vast wedge of the sea that almost split the Lemurian continent to its center, up from Tarakus the southernmost city at the end of its promontory, to Patanga at the head of the gulf, which rises at the mouth of the Twin Rvers. He had entered the gates and walked the streets unnoted by any save for Charn Thovis. And was come into the house of his only ally in all the great City of the Flame.

For Dalendus Vool, Baron of Tallan, was in secret an agent of Zaar, sworn to bring about the downfall of Patanga. Here in this house was the Black Master safe to scheme his schemes and labor furtively to bring his plan to fruition. All through those long years of painful endurance and struggle as he made his slow and torturous way across the primal continent to the gates of Patanga, his cunning brain had conceived and wrought and perfected a master plan of revenge. By now all the details were settled. The scheme was faultless. It could not fail. Thongor was doomed. Even here in the midst of his own city, ringed about with a hundred thousand warriors, the black shadow of the Last Druid would seek him out and bring him down into the dust. . . .

Days passed and the hour of the great Spring Festival was come. Gowned in festive robes, the lords of the West gathered in the mighty columned hall of the Temple of Nineteen Gods to watch the emperor make sacrifice at the high altar. Witty, sardonic, foppish young Prince Dru was there, and that bluff old warrior, Lord Mael of Tesoni, with his young daughters Inneld and Lulera. Immaculate in sparkling silver gilt harness and sky-blue cloak, Thom Pervis of the Air Guard stood beside his old comrade, Zad Komis, Lord of the Black Dragons. Prince Shangoth of the Jegga Horde loomed above the others. The calm young face of the great Nephelos, Iothondus of Kathool, could be glimpsed in the forefront of the throng, with Charn Thovis and fat old Baron Selverus and all the lesser nobility and the ambassadors from the tributary cities of Shembis and Tsargol, Zangabal and Thurdis and fair Pelorm, which had come under the banners of the empire only one year since.

With the lesser lords stood gross, unsightly Dalendus Vool, his obese bulk wrapped in gorgeous robes. Bright gems flashed at lobe and brow and breast, and his fat fingers were one dazzling shimmer of jewelry. But wealth and ostentation could not conceal the ugliness of the Baron of Tallan, for nature conspired against him from the moment of his birth. Dalendus Vool was the victim of a rare ailment which bleached his skin to a sickly pallor, faded his scant hair to silken whiteness, and gave him weak and watery eyes of unearthly pink hue. Today we call such unfortunates *albinos,* and understand their plight and sympathize with them. But to the peoples of an earlier, more barbaric and superstitious day, they were thought to be witches, and were feared and hated. As heir of a great and wealthy House, however, Dalendus Vool was saved from the contempt and fear of the commonfolk; thus was he free to come and go. But nothing eased the sick, gnawing hatred he felt for the ordinary men and women about him, more fortunate than he because of their normal pigmentation. His secret hatred ate at the roots of his being like some poisonous canker, and this flaw in his character had made him an easy victim for the wiles of Zaar, who bought his treacherous service to its cause with the tempting promise that when he had aided the Black Magicians to conquer the City of the Flame he, Dalendus Vool, would be the lord of the city, and the Patanganya his slaves to do with as his whims decreed.

It could have been noted, had any found cause to pay attention to the fact, that Dalendus Vool seemed in the grip of some powerful emotion as he stood there surrounded with his small retinue, watching the ceremonies. Sweat glistened wetly on his colorless brow and a devouring terror blazed in his sick eyes. His loose-lipped and sensuous mouth quivered and his fat bulk trembled in the intensity of his emotion. Was it fear? Or suspense? None could say, nor did any notice.

And who was that tall stranger newly come to his entourage? A lean figure, swathed in dark robes, whose hood was drawn closely about his face so that in the dim shadows where he stood none could make out his hidden features . . . naught save the glitter of emerald eyes that burned through the gloom like frozen hellfires. Thus was Mardanax of Zaar come into the very presence of his enemies.

At the altar, Thongor made offering to the Nineteen Gods whose towering figures of hewn and polished marble loomed about him in a vast semicircle—Father Gorm and smiling Tiandra, Aedir the Sungod and Illana the Moon-Lady, Karchonda of the Battles and young Iondol, Lord of Song, wise Pnoth and grim Avangra, Shastadion the Sealord and Diomala of the Harvest, and all the rest. The noon sun sent great shafts of gold light blazing through the mighty dome of glass far above. The shimmering radiance glowed softly on the smooth white marble of the towering, heroic figures of the gods, and one shaft fell on the altar itself, catching Thongor the Lord of the West in its brilliant ray.

A burley-thewed, bronze lion of a man was this barbarian adventurer from the far Northlands who had come brawling and battling through half the cities of the South until some plan of the gods of whim of that destiny men say rule even the gods had lifted him to a high place among the kings of the earth. Although robed in splendid cloth of gold, his magnificent body could be seen, by breadth of shoulder and depth of chest, to be thewed like some savage gladiator. Still in the full prime of his manhood, kingship and luxury had not dulled his superb fighting skill nor softened his iron strength.

His grim, impassive face was an expressionless mask of hard dark bronze, majestic and stern beneath the rude mane of coarse thick black hair that poured over his massive back and heavy shoulders and was held from his face by a glorious circlet of fiery diamonds set in a crown of opalescent jazite metal. Under scowling black brows his strange gold eyes blazed with savage power like the eyes of a kingly and untamed lion of the jungles. For this state occasion, he had set aside this once the great Valkarthan broadsword that seldom left his side. Such a man was Thongor in the noontide of his mighty prime, the greatest warrior of all his age, hero of a thousand legends, who had cut a crimson path through a thousand perils to win a throne beside the woman he loved.

It was in this moment when Thongor stood at the height of his glory that Mardanax of Zaar struck him down.

For seven nights the masked magician had readied himself for this titanic moment when he should unleash the full force of his dark sorcery against his most hated enemy. The crypts and catacombs beneath the palace of Dalendus Vool had witnessed many grim and terrible scenes of torment and punishment, but none so awful as the black rites wherewith the Black Druid prepared himself for the hour of his triumph. Each dawn the rushing waters of the Twin Rivers bore out to sea on their floods the obscenely mutilated corpses of certain slaves from whose skin the

21

ownership-mark of Tallan's baron had been removed . . . pitiful cadavers whose life-force, brutally torn from agonized flesh, had been offered up by Mardanax in sacrifice to the Triple Lord of Chaos.

Power was his now for a time, great power, power to strike and slay with a terrific blast of magic force. Once he had stood among the Nine Wizards of Zaar, who each were a pole of power and, united, formed a nucleus of tremendous force upon the earth. Now his comrades were gone and his power diminished vastly by the sundering of those astral bonds and currents which flowed between the nine poles. Yet, for a time, a borrowed power was his. And with this withering blast he struck down the Lord of the West there at the mighty altar of the gods.

Terror and consternation flamed through the throng as Thongor fell lifeless at the altar's base. Nobles paled, gasping with shock, staring the one at the other with astonishment and horror. Women shrieked and swooned. Guards roared commands, baring bright steel as if the strength of swords alone could serve to defend the royal family of Patanga against the unseen assault of magic-working foes.

Amid the surging crowds of shouting, cursing, praying men and women, none were unmoved. Even Dalendus Vool, privy to the plot from its inception, stood with ghastly fear written on his wet and flabby features. Only the gaunt form of the masked one was calm, aloof, and unshaken, gloating triumph stamped on his veiled and hidden features. His slitted eyes of emerald flame blazed with unholy joy as he watched Princess Sumia weeping heartbrokenly over the motionless form of her beloved warrior. One by one they took their places about the fallen King, Zad Komis, Prince Dru, Selverus and Lord Mael, Shangoth of the Jegga, young Iothondus and the rest of Thongor's staunchest comrades.

Only Charn Thovis held back from joining their circle. The young warrior, a recent member of the Black Dragons, even more recently elevated by Thongor to the rank of kojan of the empire, felt he had not the right to intrude on the private sorrow of the dead king's closest friends.

Thus was he in a position to notice the tall, dark-robed

figure in the retinue of Dalendus Vool, and to note how the personage of hidden face stood unshaken and calm amidst the restless throng. Where had he seen such a figure before? Only days before had he looked upon a strange man, robed and hooded and unknown. Could this noble servitor to the Baron of Tallan be that furtive and tattered beggar who had accosted him at the gates with dawn those fifteen days ago?

The young warrior in the leather harness of the Black Dragons stood staring curiously at the hooded figure, and a thoughtful expression furrowed his brows as he stared. As for the masked magician, he did not notice the young chanthar at all; Mardanax of Zaar was too busy drinking in the intoxicating glory of this, his great moment of triumph and victory. He was too deeply entranced in the spectacle before his eyes to spare a single glance for Charn Thovis. He was to regret this in the days to come. For the young and noble warrior was to remember that motionless figure, and was to dwell upon it in his thoughts through the events of the coming days.

Chapter 3: THE SECRET COUNCIL

> When coils of dark conspiracy
> Through secret traitors grip the land,
> Those loyal men who would be free
> Must rise and take a stand.
>
> —*The Scarlet Edda*

The stone fortress of Sardath Keep rises in the green hills of the Tesoni lordship to the north of Patanga where the two rivers of the Saan and the Ysar part, the one to curve away westward into the lush jungle country of Chush, the other to find a path through the vast and mighty Mountains of Mommur that run the length of the continent of ancient Lemuria like a mountainous spine.

Here for seven hundred years the lordly ancestors of Lord Mael dwelt in baronial splendor.

Here in the hour of midnight, by furtive and stealthy and secret ways, came ten men summoned to a hasty conference by the Lord Mael.

Besides Mael himself, there came fat old Baron Selverus, second of the three peers of the realm. But Prince Dru was absent. He was immured in the palace and inaccessible. Likewise absent for much the same reason was old Thom Pervis, Daotar of the Air Guard, although his friend Zad Komis was here with Iothondus and Prince Shangoth and aged Father Eodrym, Hierarch of the Temple of Nineteen Gods. Young Charn Thovis had also come.

The ten made their path to Sardath Keep by devious ways, some like Selverus and Eodrym and Iothondus overland by zamph or kroter. Others, like Shangoth and Zad Komis, came by air in private floaters, as the weird and magical sky boats of the ancient Lemurians were called. They met in secret, for dark and desperate times had come upon the Empire of the West in the seven days that had passed since the sudden and tragic death of their friend and monarch, Thongor of Valkarth.

Almost from the very moment the body of Thongor, clad in his leathern war harness, wrapped in his mighty crimson cloak, with the great Valkarthan broadsword clasped against the cold flesh of his breast, was laid to rest in a sepulchre of white marble built before the high altar of the temple—strange events had begun to occur.

Sumia, his incomparable young queen, withdrew into the seclusion of the palace and was seldom seen in public again. She inexplicably dissolved the council of advisers who had well and faithfully served Thongor in the years of his reign, assuming total power in her own person—which, under the laws of Patanga, she was certainly entitled to do, but nonetheless her action in this matter was odd, and seemed uncalled for.

Next, as the heir, Prince Thar, was only nine years old, the Sarkaja had selected a Prince Regent to govern the realm in her name and that of her son. Again she had acted in a most strange and discomforting manner, passing over her most trusted peers to select none other than Dalendus Vool, a minor kojan of the lesser nobility rarely seen at court and as much disliked as he was distrusted. In a single stroke, the Baron of Tallan was become the first peer of the realm.

Ominous and inexplicable actions had followed thereafter one upon the other so swiftly that Lord Mael and the others hardly knew from one day to the next where matters stood. Sumia's only living relative, her cousin Prince Dru, had vanished into the palace and become incommunicado. Had he perhaps been imprisoned on some vague charge—was this unseemly event *possible?* Alas, in such darkening and troublous times, it was all too possible, for many high-placed men of long and proven loyalty to the throne had been jailed and were jailed to this hour. Among them, most sadly, was gallant old Thom Pervis, one of Patanga's greatest warriors and, as Daotar of the Air Guard, one of the most important commanders of the legions that shielded the empire from its enemies. Dalendus Vool had demanded the old officer surrender himself on flimsy and trumped-up charges, and the loyal Daotar had complied—for, incredibly, the order for his imprisonment was countersigned with the signature and seal of Sumia Sarkaja herself!

Matters like these, dubious and uncertain, clouded with mystery, had brought the ten men together in this remote castle for a council. Now was the time to confer, to draw inferences and to plan a course of action, for who among them could be certain that tomorrow *he* would not be imprisoned in the dungeons beneath the mighty palace on some unlikely charge?

Thus had Mael dispatched the most loyal warriors of his Tesoni clan to the far corners of the empire to summon in secret session those proven friends of Sumia and Thongor. Hither flew Ald Turmis, Sark of Shembis, the third city of the empire, and one of Thongor's oldest friends and fighting companions. But the messenger entrusted with a summons to Karm Karvus, another of the Valkarthan's most valiant comrades, seemed to have gone astray. For neither did he return from that red-walled city of Tsargo, fourth city of the empire, that rose on the wave-lashed shores of Yashengzeb Chun the Southern Sea where Karm Karvus had ruled as Sark these past eight years, nor did Karm Karvus arrive for the council, as he most surely would, had the message reached him.

And from Thudis, second city of the empire, the old Sark Barand Thon sent his stalwart young son, the Jasark Ramchan Thon, as his accredited representative. From Zangabal came Prince Zul, younger brother of the Sark of that city. Zangabal had joined the empire of its own free will four years ago. But no word came from the Sark of Pelorm; again, as in the case of seacoast Tsargol, a messenger must have gone astray or failed to reach his goal for some more ominous reason. . . .

Lord Mael admitted that he found the actions of Sumia Sarkaja incomprehensible. "It is as if the lass had turned against us all," he growled, hunching his beefy shoulders and shaking his massive head like a baffled and angry old bear.

"The most puzzling of her actions, to my mind, is this singling out of the Baron of Tallan as regent," Ald Turmis said. "To pass over such elder advisers and friends of long-proven loyalty as the Lord Mael or Baron Selverus or Prince Dru, in favor of a little known and even less liked kojan such as this Dalendus Vool is simply incredible," he mused in a puzzled tone.

The young philosopher Iothondus nodded agreement. "She is like one under the spell of some potent drug," he said thoughtfully. "At first I believed her erratic actions the result of shock and sorrow. Now I wonder . . . the steps the Sarkaja has taken these past few days are so unlike her normal state of mind that she resembles one acting according to the dictates of a superior will. It is as if she is under some enchantment."

That doughty old warrior, Zad Komis, growled his

agreement. One horny palm grasped the well-worn pommel of his rapier and his keen eyes flashed. "If the Queen needs our aid, we must come to her assistance and free her from whatever force has bound her!" he said harshly.

Heads nodded about the table, but Mael summed up their common doubt. "But who can we strike against—who is the enemy? Or is there in fact no enemy, except in our imaginations? What if the lass is under no dominance but simply acting of her own wishes—how then can we protest? How can we *know?*"

Many more words were spoken and many other subjects brought under scrutiny and discussion, but when at dawn the council broke up and the ten dispersed each to his home, nothing had been concluded.

The lords of the empire were baffled, worried, suspicious and angry, but they could find no enemy to strike out against, no evidence of treason or of foul play.

They left Sardath Keep as the first rays of dawn struck rose and golden fire from the upper peaks of the Mountains of Mommur and lit the clouds of heaven to brilliant flame. They agreed to keep on the alert and in touch with one another, to watch and listen and be wary. That seemed to be all that they could do. So cleverly had the secret foes of Patanga manipulated the current of events that they remained faceless and hidden.

But one of the ten was filled with a grim determination to do something, to take some positive action. Charn Thovis had contributed little to the council. He felt unworthy to speak up and to voice his thoughts in the presence of his senior peers. But in his mind was one course of action that could be initiated: one of them must break the seclusion wherein Sumia was kept, even if her privacy was a matter of her own wishes. One must confront her with these and other questions, and make certain that the Sarkaja was not somehow under the power of an enemy.

Charn Thovis resolved to be that man.

Chapter 4: THE FLYING MAN

> Thus doom hath struck and Thongor dies.
> On substanceless and airy wing
> His soul ascends beyond the skies,
> Where Death the Conqueror is King.
>
> What of the realm he leaves behind?
> What of his lovely, lonely Queen?
> Dark traitors subtly sway her mind,
> Twixt her and old friends come between.
>
> —*Thongor's Saga*, Stave XVIII

Night hung like a canopy of black velvet over Patanga. Thick vapors hid the great golden moon of old Lemuria and veiled the host of her attendant stars. The City of the Flame was cloaked in darkness and thick fog rolled in from the gulf to fill her broad stone-paved avenues and squares with dense mists.

Above the royal city, silvery airboats circled tirelessly and keen-eyed officers of the Air Guard kept watch through the long hours of the night. Over the Great Plaza at the city's heart the floaters drove, above the Temple of the Nineteen Gods and the mighty Thorian Way that stretched from the central square to the West Gate. Over the bazaar and the Hierarchal Palace and above the Palace of Sarks, where it lay amidst the dark shrubbery of the parks and gardens that encircled it.

Neither the guards stationed at gate or tower-top or palace door saw the weird figure that drifted through the black skies toward the palace wherein Sumia dwelt.

A gust of wind arose over the waters and stirred the languid banners of black and gold. For a moment the thick mists that hung above the old stone city were torn asunder and the gold moon peered through them on the slumbering city.

For a moment the flying figure was silhouetted against the bright shield of the moon. Manlike it was, enveloped in what appeared to be vast floating wings. The moment passed; clouds again obscured the night sky. The dark form was again invisible to view.

Silent as a drifting autumn leaf, the flying man came to light upon a balcony of carven marble which obtruded from a tower of the palace far above the fog-drenched gardens. A gloved hand reached for the handle of the long windows. They opened and a dark cloaked figure slid between heavy curtains and vanished within the palace.

The halls of the palace were deserted at this late hour. Only an occasional guard, leaning upon the shaft of his spear, stood at stations here and there throughout the upper stories of the vast structure. But in the private suites reserved for the royal family, guards were few.

The dark figure slunk on silent feet down an immense hall. Superb tapestries of ancient workmanship displayed in somber hues the amours of gods and heroes. Alabaster statues and busts of long-dead monarchs stood enshrined in niches along the corridor. Light blazed from candelabra, twinkling on vases of precious metals. Through empty halls and silent apartments the dark figure crept. A black cloak was drawn about it. A hood concealed the features in shadow.

At the great door of Princess Sumia's suite, the cloaked figure paused and bent to listen. No sound came from within. No guard was stationed here, for Dalendus Vool wished to make it impossible for *any* person to have converse or to pass any message to the Sarkaja. Hence the guardposts had been rearranged. Guards stood at the head of each stair which led to the level whereon the royal suites were established. In this way, the Baron of Tallan made it impossible—or so he thought—for any to communicate with the Sarkaja, since to reach her apartments a

29

messenger would have to enter the palace and pass a score of guardposts in his ascent to this high level.

Neither Dalendus Vool nor his dark master had envisioned the possibility of an interloper arriving from the sky.

At the door, Charn Thovis cast his hood back and entered with a key supplied him by the Lady Inneld. Inneld, daughter of Lord Mael, had been Sumia's handmaiden until her dismissal a few days before. Dalendus Vool had removed all of Sumia's servants, replacing them with his own staff. But Inneld had retained her private key and on the urgings of Charn Thovis had given it to the young chanthar.

He entered stealthily, knowing that this act could result in his arrest or death. These apartments were forbidden to all on pain of direst punishment. And if the Sarkaja were to raise the alarm he could give no good reason for his secret entry into the palace nor for his unlawful presence in the private suite of the queen and the young prince. However, he felt the risk worth taking.

Hence he had prevailed upon Iothondus for the philosopher's assistance. The sage of Kathool had recently been experimenting with a new invention—a new use of the magic metal urlium, the weird alloy that resisted the force of gravity and fell up instead of down. This antigravitic metal was the secret which enabled the flying airboats of Patanga to resist the pull of their own weight. The mage had perfected a flying harness covered with plates of the curious glistening metal. This harness, which Iothondus called "the skybelt," was precisely counterbalanced to the weight of the human body, rendering its wearer perfectly weightless. Wearing the skybelt, a man could float through the air, propelling himself for considerable distances by his muscular strength.

Charn Thovis had found that an ordinary leap could carry him fifty paces into the air, sustaining his weight for a distance of two hundred yards. Wearing the skybelt, then, and cloaked and visored in black against chance notice by any watchful eye, he had hurled himself into empty air from the rooftop of an adjoining mansion . . . and floated like a weightless cloud into the upper works of the palace.

Within the Sarkaja's suite, he found empty rooms in darkness. Was the queen asleep? Daring much, he made a light. He was in an antechamber adjoining the main suite. Cautiously, he entered the suite and paced silently through the gorgeously appointed rooms. On the threshold of the sleeping chamber he paused, again listening. No sound came to his straining sense. He went in, lifting the candelabra before him. It cast a wavering sphere of illumination over the bedroom. And he saw what he had come to see.

Fully clothed, motionless as an eidolon of polished marble, Sumia Sarkaja sat upright in a great gilded chair. Her eyes were open and stared directly ahead, but did not turn upon Charn Thovis as he entered the room. Her breast rose in slow, shallow breathing, almost imperceptible to the eye. It was that alone told him she still lived.

"My lady!" he gasped, and came to his knees by her side—but she stirred not, neither did she deign to notice him. She continued staring at the empty air as if totally unaware of his presence. He touched her hand where it lay limp and lifeless upon the arm of the chair. It was cool to the touch—like a thing fashioned from pale wax.

"My lady? Do you know me?" he whispered. She made no reply of any kind; her gaze remained fixed on emptiness and did not waver even when he moved his hand before her eyes.

Charn Thovis was puzzled—frightened. He felt a nameless foreboding well up within his heart. Something was wrong here . . . something was terribly wrong! He bent his attention upon her more closely. The warm vivid colors had fled from her face, leaving it pale and serene as a waxen mask. No animation lit her splendid dark eyes that the bards had oft compared to wet glistening black jewels. Her body seemed alive but—untenanted.

Then there came to his nostrils a sickly, overpowering odor. A thick musky sweetness, heady and overripe. The dense perfume made his senses swim.

With a thrill of pure horror he recognized that mind-dulling fragrance. It was the perfume of a potent narcotic called nothlaj, the Flower of Dreams, a drug which submerged the mind of its user in rosy visions, and bent his will to the dominance of others. Charn Thovis muffled an expletive as his mind recoiled from this awful discovery. In a flash, the full extent of the secret plot against the crown of Patanga was revealed to him as he stood there astounded and quivering with revulsion.

Some stealthy and cunning traitor had utilized the evil properties of this loathsome narcotic to dull the wits of the Sarkaja and to render her totally subservient. No wonder her actions since the death of Thongor had seemed like the acts of another—no wonder she had dissolved the council of her advisers and withdrew from their surveillance into full privacy! Whatever clever mentality was behind this plot knew full well that the effects of nothlaj could not be easily concealed from the intelligent eye. Only in secret, where she could be commanded to set her signature and seal upon subversive acts and writs and messages, could the traitors manipulate her and hide behind her. In public appearances, her condition would be exposed in an instant. No wonder, then, that Dalendus Vool had dismissed her attendants, replacing them with hand-picked servitors of his own party.

The full extent of this treason smote Charn Thovis as he stood there, staggering under the incredible implications. Whoever was behind this plot—whether Dalendus Vool or another—was now in absolute control of the city and empire of Patanga. Through his total control over the Sarkaja, he could commit any enormity without risk of detection!

A sudden thought struck Charn Thovis as he stood there wondering what to do. The queen was beyond his aid—but what of the young prince, her son? Had Prince Thar eluded the traitor's cunning hand—or was the boy, too, in the awful power of the devilish nothlaj?

The apartments of the Jasark adjoined those of his mother. Charn Thovis entered them, lifting the candelabra, to see the lad rousing from normal healthy slumber, rubbing his eyes against the light.

"Charn Thovis!" the boy exclaimed, his eyes widening. "What are *you* doing here?"

Charn Thovis spoke on sheer impulse, without premeditation. "I've come to take you to Lord Mael for a visit."

The boy's eyes—so like the strange gold eyes of his father—sparkled with excitement.

"Will I be able to see Lady Inneld and Lady Lulera again?" he asked. "I've missed them so much! Will Lord Mael let me ride on a kroter again? They haven't let me out of the palace for *days!*"

Charn Thovis' jaw tightened grimly. "Yes, son, you can ride on a kroter and play with your nurses again," he said absently. His mind was racing. Above all loomed the question of *what to do?* As the lad rose and skinned off his nightclothes, strapping a miniature warrior's harness about his lean and sturdy young body, Charn Thovis stood thinking.

There did not seem to be anything he could do to save the Queen. His flying harness might be able to support the boy's light weight, but he knew it would not bear up the additional weight of a full-grown woman. Hence he could not rescue both the drugged queen and her son. What, then, should he do? It was an agonizing decision and he had little time to think it out. For all he knew, the queen was so fully under the control of her enemies' will that to take her from them now might cause her death from the psychic severence. On the other hand, in the person of Prince Thar lay the succession of the throne and the future of the empire. Charn Thovis made his choice with an unspoken prayer that he had chosen wisely.

The boy was almost ready. He tied a scarlet loincloth about his hips and settled his cloak about his shoulders, clipping to the girdle of his harness a small sword given to him by his dead father. Charn Thovis saw in the husky, sturdy nine-year-old, with his coarse black mane and scowling brows and strange gold eyes, the mirror-image of his mighty sire. And tears stung Charn Thovis' eyes until he shrugged them away.

"I'm ready, Charn Thovis! Shall I say goodbye to Mother?" the lad asked eagerly.

"No, my Prince. Your mother is . . . asleep. Come!" He

tossed back his cloak and adjusted the glittering harness. A powered sithurl was set in the chestplate. A touch to its control-nodes would energize the urlium plating, rendering him and the boy nearly weightless. The boy's eyes sparkled with excitement.

"A skybelt! I've heard of those, but my father said I was too young to fly with one. My father said it was too dangerous—"

A lump formed in Charn Thovis' throat to hear the lad speak of his dead sire. The warrior vowed silently that he would move heaven and earth to shield this precious seed of Thongor's mighty line from harm. The first step was to waft him from the very stronghold of his enemies, and spirit him away to a secret hiding place among the ten loyalists. Then the banners of revolution could be lifted and the perfidy of Dalendus Vool proclaimed across the land, raising an army of vengeance to support the succession of Prince Thar and unseat the vile usurper that abode now in the seat of stolen power. . . .

"Come, Prince," he said, scooping the lad up in his arms. Settling the boy upon his back, locking the lad's arms about his throat and cautioning him to hold on tight, Charn Thovis energized the skybelt and sprang through the window into the dark night.

Friendless and alone, ringed about with their enemies, the loyal warrior and the young prince vanished in the darkness. The hope and the future of Patanga rode on Charn Thovis' broad shoulders as he launched forth into the empty darkness and flew away into the night.

The Second Book

THONGOR IN THE LAND OF SHADOWS

"Know, O mortal, that beyond these Lands of the Living there lieth that far and mysterious realm wherein the shadows dwell. Strange and awesome beyond belief are the marvels and mysteries of the Shadowlands, wherein naught is what it seems and thy lonely spirit wanders for eternity amidst the symbols and cryptic analogues of this life ere yet thou dost venture on into the next. Here the very Gods move among the shades of men and thou standest in the stupendous Presence before whom art thou judged for all time to come. . . ."

—*The Scarlet Edda*

Chapter 5: THE DWELLER ON THE
THRESHOLD

> The Shadow-Gates before him loom,
> Grim gateways of eternal stone
> Beyond the shadows of the tomb,
> Strange portals to a land unknown . . .

> —*Thongor's Saga,* Stave XVIII

After an immeasurable gulf of time, Thongor found himself standing before the towering arch of some stupendous gate. All about him beat great winds and his ears rang with distant wailing voices whose words he could not make out. He stared up at the soaring pylons of the gate and strove to comprehend what had happened to him. All he remembered was a searing thrust of pain against his heart—then naught but an abyss of whirling dark and howling gales and biting cold that cut to the marrow. Then . . . nothingness . . . until he regained his senses to find himself standing in the very shadow of this titanic gate.

It was hewn from some bright metal or glistening stone, and it shimmered in his gaze with such supernal brilliance that he could not fully focus his vision upon it. The arch seemed taller than the tallest tower of his city of Patanga, and its surfaces were sculpted all over with seething multitudes of human figures. There were weeping women and battling youths, and old men stretched out upon their beds as if at the moment of death, with veiled figures about them, and youths and maidens playing, crowned kings and tattered beggars, corpulent lords at feast and sly, grinning thieves, crones and babes and all forms of mortality.

"Thou dost gaze upon the Gate between the Worlds, O Man!"

The voice was deep and sonorous and of unearthly resonance, such as sounded never from a human breast. He started and half-turned, one hand darting to his hip where it should have clasped the hard pommel of a great Valkarthan broadsword, but instead it brushed bare flesh. And looking down he was astonished to find that he was naked as on the day of his birth.

"Who speaks?" he demanded, and the sound of his voice over the wind sounded strange in his ears, as if it was not his voice at all.

"I, who dwell here from one eternity unto the next, upon the threshold of this realm whereunto thou hast come at last, as all men come in the fullness of time."

Peering closer, Thongor saw that within the arch of the gigantic gate sat a strange figure. Seated, it still was taller than ever was mortal man. From head to foot, the titanic figure was veiled in some dark stuff that was not cloth, at least not any cloth he knew. It was as if darkness itself clothed the curious figure of the Dweller on the Threshold.

Fighting against the raging gale, Thongor strode nearer until he came to stand before the veiled one. Wrathful fires stirred in his lion-bright eyes and anger, mixed with awe and a dim shadow of fear, rose within his breast.

"What is this place," he growled, "and how have I come here—and who or what are you who hold this gate?"

The figure robed and hooded in shadows shook its mighty head ponderously, and there was a hint of mockery in its deep, solemn voice as it spoke again.

"Questions and yet more questions, yet always the same questions!" the voice mocked him gently. *"O Man, look behind thee and tell me what thou seest."*

Thongor turned to look behind—and felt his reason reel! Behind him the world fell away like a mighty cliff . . . aye, the great-grandfather of all cliffs, for so deeply did the walls fall away that the bottom thereof was thick and black with shadows . . . shadows wherein he was weirdly shaken to see *stars* glitter! Stars blazed far at the uttermost bottom of the vast abyss!

He lifted his dazed and uncomprehending eyes and stared across the dim and mystic gulf. On the other side— the gods alone knew how far away!—he glimpsed a tableland, a plateau or level land so vast that his gaze could encompass whole oceans in their entirety upon it, aye, and the enormous width of continents unknown to him. And amongst them, he dimly glimpsed the familiar outlines of that mighty Lemuria he had left. He could see the dull, glistening wedge of the gulf cutting deep into the center of the continent, but from this enormous height and colossal distance the great city of Patanga itself was only the tiniest of flecks, invisible to his eyes that blurred and watered against the screaming wings of the storm.

Clouds hung above it, moving slowly. Half the land was in daylight, half drenched in night's ebon gloom.

The moon, the mighty moon, far below him, was a small gold globe. The stars hung close and low over the vast world as his eyes saw it.

Between that world and this stretched the dim enormity of the Abyss. Between the worlds, streaming up from the Lands of the Living unto where he stood on the shores of Never were a dim and flickering host of shadows in constant motion, streaming between the worlds. Even as he stood staring down, they flashed by him, through the stupendous Shadow-Gates, some weeping, some crying out to friends, some praying, some laughing madly, some silent, with bowed head and clasped hands.

"Thou knowest now that thou art dead and come hither unto the Shadowlands," the Dweller observed.

Thongor growled deep in his massive chest. His grim impassive face was flushed and somber. Anger flamed in his strange gold eyes. He shook his head, tousling his streaming mane.

"Dead? Not I! How came I unto death?" he growled. "No foeman's blade brought me down, no winged arrow, no poison in the cup. In the prime of manhood was I, no doddering and senile grandsire—how then came I to death? Answer me, if you can, O Dweller!"

The enshadowed one shook its head again. *"There are more mysteries between Life and Death than mortals dare*

38

to dream. *No god am I, and thus I dare not speak the reasons for thy death, O Man.*"

Thongor stared down at his hands, his arms, his broad chest. Surely they were flesh and blood, as they seemed to his sight! And yet—and yet he felt strange, as if his bare flesh was insensitive, as if his sense of feeling was numbed or had become a faint echo of itself. He could not feel the rough cold stone underfoot, not the fingers of the wind along his bare flanks. Before he could voice the question that rose within him, the Dweller spake, answering it.

"*Here, all things are but illusion. Thou are a bodiless spirit, but to thine sight thine own self is an analogue of thy earthly being. Go hence, O Man, and roam amongst the Shadowlands until thou hast found the reality and canst see beyond the semblance to the true.*"

Thongor gazed upon the fantastic figure cloaked in shadows, and he searched within himself to understand the other's speech.

"What must I seek?" he demanded. "Speak more clearly, ancient one, and have done with these vague utterances, I beseech you!"

The Dweller smiled behind his shadows.

"*Aye, then here is thy quest in terms as clear as I am permitted to make them. Thou shalt wander the Land of Shadows until thou comest before the Throne of Thrones, O Mortal . . . and ere that time comes upon thee, thou shalt master the Three Truths.*"

Slowly the Dweller faded from Thongor's sight.

What were the Three Truths? How, in this misty realm of strangeness, could he discern truth from illusion? How could he know which truths were meant for him to search out and to learn? *Was ever a mortal man given a task such as this, whether in the Land of the Living or the Realm of Death?*

Thongor went forward, dazed and uncomprehending. He passed under the enormous glittering arch of the Shadow-Gates and he found himself on the threshold of a strange new world of dim horizons and vast perspectives, where no object or shape or form could be seen plainly. All were queer shadowy semblances, visible only in an oblique manner; they defied a straight gaze and somehow eluded his vision, twisting away in a way he could neither quite sense nor understand nor even describe.

As he went forward through the purple gloom, his dazed mind was busy, grappling with strange thoughts. He knew that he must be dead . . . but his innate courage, his warrior's fighting spirit that could not acknowledge defeat, revolted against the thought. And *was* he dead? He pondered the elusive, ambiguous words of the Dweller.

Always had he been told that when the valiant fell, the winged War-Maids bore them on throbbing pinions far above the world and beyond the stars through the infinite to the glittering Hall of Heroes where the great of the earth dwelt ever before Father Gorm. But he had not come into the Land of Shadows in this manner, nor were these the Shining Fields nor the Halls of Gorm. Where, then, was the truth of the myth?

He set the mystery of his present state aside for further thought.

If dead he were in truth, then his lovely queen and his young son were alone and bereft in that distant world behind him. He was shaken to the core of his being by this thought, but somehow the emotion did not seem fully real. He should have been crushed with anguish and loss and sorrow, bowed under the grim knowledge that never would he behold the fair face of his beloved, nor clasp her yielding slimness in his strong arms again, and taste the warmth of her lips under his kiss . . . but somehow he felt only the *shadow* of sorrow, not the poignant agony of heart and soul he should have felt.

He pondered this, and was aware that his emotions were but dim echoes of the heart-shaking throes he would have felt in the body. If this spirit-form was but the shadow of his mortal body, then it naturally followed that his emotions would be shadow-emotions—dim imitations of the strong realities. A weird world, this, and a strange state of being.

He surveyed his surroundings. He moved across a dim plain drowned in thick purple shadows. To all sides, the

40

plain stretched away bleak and barren and desolate, devoid of life. Winds blew above this plain, moaning like lost souls, but his heavy black mane did not stir to the wind's caress. It was the shadow of a wind . . . or his mane was but the shadow of matter, and wind could not touch it.

There was a dull crystalline sand under his feet. But it did not crunch and rasp beneath his step. Was he walking in truth, or progressing by some weird mode of bodiless locomotion, which his dreaming mind interpreted as walking? Was this desert real, or only a ghostly illusion?

His body was bare and seemed his own, but it felt eerily light of weight and impalpable to the touch. It did not have the warm solidity and weight of true flesh. From this, then, he deduced that his spirit-self was the exact Shadowlands counterpart of his earthly envelope of clay—and he himself was but the insubstantial analogue of his mortal form. Strange to realize one's death has come and past! In one swift moment of time, all earthly cares and responsibilities are shorn away—fading behind as if they had never been real at all, and one is thrust into a strange new world.

He looked about him. On all sides, a level plain of dark flat sand stretched away to a dim horizon. Here no strong light beat, no burning sun lit up a sky of mystic purple gloom wherein no stars blazed, nor was there any moon.

Here and there about the vast plain rose curious shapes of rough-hewn stone. Were they naught but jagged shapes of uncouth rock, or were they statues of some alien artistry, curious and geometrical and hauntingly unfamiliar? He lingered to examine the nearer of the dark eidolons. It was shapen into the caricature of a man, ungainly and inhumanly tall and gaunt with elongated limbs whose sharply angled segments emerged from the rough surface of the monolith. The limbs were vague and blurred, as if some sculptor of incredible skill had striven to suggest a body wrapped and veiled in clinging mists. The head that loomed above the gaunt form was totally unlike anything human, a perfect cone devoid of any features remotely manlike.

Except for the eyes.

A vague unease traveled up Thongor's spine as he perceived that the graven eyes of the alien image seemed to regard him with bright mockery as he passed. Some trick of light and shade, no doubt, but they seemed *alive* . . . and conscious.

He hurried on, careful to avoid similar eidolons for the rest of his journey.

Winds blew above the measureless plain, although he felt them not. Faint far sounds came dimly to him as he wandered. He thought he heard calling voices beseeching, now and again a repeated name, an urgent phrase. None of this could he hear clearly and although he often paused and strained to hear, he could not make out a single word or name.

Now and again came cries of pain, the sounds of imploring voices raised in unendurable torment or longing . . . and at times he thought he heard a strange burst of mocking laughter, clear and cold. It was unspeakably weird and he forced his thoughts from the unbodied drifting voices, knowing that here on the unending plains were other presences beyond his own, and far, far stranger.

A shadow passed overhead and he ducked in a chill of alarm. But when he looked up he could see nothing except coiling ropes of mist which writhed slowly far above, forming wavering tentacles and serpent-shapes, and now and again eddying into the likeness of a glaring eye or a grinning mouth or a long undulating limb. He tore his eyes from the strange vista above, and plodded on.

Time seemed meaningless in this dim land. There was neither night nor day nor any way of telling the passage of the hours. He felt neither hunger nor thirst, nor did the long journey fatigue his mighty limbs. It might have been one hour or a hundred hours—or even a hundred years—later when he suddenly came upon the ring of stones.

He had been striding mechanically along, busy with vague thoughts, paying little attention to the path. Indeed, he did not truly know where he was going, in what direction or toward what far goal, nor had he thought to ask.

Abruptly he became conscious of a vertical surface rising before him. He stopped and looked ahead, peering through the purple gloom. Ahead of him, in a vast circle, seven mighty slabs of dark and glistening stone stood on the edges about some bright glittering object within the center of their ring.

A dim premonition stirred his dull dreaming wits. He must go cautiously in this strange realm of the dead. Gorm alone knew what terrors and marvels moved about him, veiled from his sight. He peered curiously at the ring of stones. The gaps between the stones were wide, but somehow he sensed a warning. The stones were set here for a purpose, either to keep something out . . . or to hold something within.

He knew that he must resolve this mystery before passing on. So gathering his powers in readiness, he moved forward cautiously until he entered the ring of stones.

For a moment a strange impalpable barrier seemed to hold him back. He could see nothing before him but he could not move forward. It was as if a wall of curdled shadows opposed his path. Gathering his strength, and mentally calling on Father Gorm for aid, he pressed forward, and found the barrier melting before him.

He stepped forward fully into the ring, and saw—

Chapter 6:   THE SWORD IN THE JEWEL

> His soul hath passed the Shadow-Gates
> And ventures on a nameless quest.
> A stranger destiny awaits
> Him here than even he hath guessed!
>
> —*Thongor's Saga*, Stave XVIII

A Titanic jewel! Taller than a man it loomed, hewn into a thousand glassy facets, flashing with light. In all this dim and unsubstantial Land of Shadows he had seen no brighter thing than this great glittering boulder of cut light.

The crystal was lucent as ice, a pallid blue like summery seas. Rough-hewn it towered, like some mighty iceberg from the wintry waves of Zharanga Tethrabaal the Great North Ocean. A cluster, a focus of dazzling rays, shone from it in beams of glowing radiance.

About it marched the ring of seven stones, like giants set to guard its precious brilliance . . . giants petrified to stone though long aeons of slow-pulsing time.

He stood staring at the jewel. There was something uncanny about it—some current of queer force that roughened his bronze hide and set his nape-hairs prickling in superstitious awe. For all his years among the civilized folk who dwelt in the great cities of the West, Thongor was a primitive still, with all the barbarian's night-terrors and sense of omens.

To set down his mental impressions in mere words were a futile task, for they were but inarticulate surges of emotion—a tingling of the nerve-endings, the eerie stirrings of vague premonitions, no more.

Somehow, he sensed the Thing in the circle was the most truly *real* object he had yet spied in all this weird realm of the spirit-world. In truth, what were the cryptic words the Dweller on the Threshold spake?—*Here, all things are but illusion . . . go hence, and roam the Shadowlands . . . until thou seest beyond the semblance to the true. . . .*

He stepped forward to peer more closely into the titanic jewel. Light beat from it in shimmering beams. He found it oddly difficult to move against the flowing rays of luminance—as if impalpable barriers rose before him to obstruct his passage nearer to the jewel. Naught that he could see nor feel, naught sensible to touch or vision. He felt as one enmeshed in the dim webs of some unearthly spider.

Setting his jaw with grim determination, and again hurling forth an unvoiced prayer to Gorm, Father of Earth and Heaven, he moved against the shimmering curtain of semivisible force and felt it drag almost imperceptibly against his bare limbs as he strove to penetrate the net of shining beams.

Now he had come up to the jewel.

He peered within, through glimmering panes and flashing angles, his gaze sinking through the translucent crystal into far depths of throbbing indigo flame where sparkling atoms of utter light danced like elfin flakes of supernal fire.

He saw the Sword.

It lay imbedded deep within the glittering crystal. Indigo flame coiled and seethed about its shining length. Stars of scintillance blazed and flashed on its mighty pommel. It was sunken into the very center of the mystic jewel, as sometimes in his boyhood he had seen great mastodons deep frozen within the sparkling walls of a vast glacier.

No mortal weapon was this, surely, for his hand had clasped the hilts of all manner of human weaponry. Seven feet long the great blade extended from the mighty cross-shaped hilt. Nor was that keen blade forged from any metal known to the smiths of men, nay, for mirror-bright it blazed—some pure and glistening alloy worked by Aslak the God-Smith, or by some fabled race of beings who had trod the earth aeons before the coming of men.

His hand yearned to close about the great hilt, to heft the mighty weight of the sword, to test the unearthly temper of its blazing edge.

He knew he must free the sword from its crystal prison. How he knew this he could not put into words, but the unspoken conviction seethed up from deep within him and he knew it must be done. Perhaps the sword was set here in this place from the Dawn of the Created Universe for him to take up in this moment. Perhaps the gods had written into the tablets of the destiny of Thongor that he take up this potent and supernatural blade. He knew not . . . but he knew the sword was his, and that he must free it.

With such as Thongor, grim men of direct and frontal action, not given to subleties of thought, to think is to act. He moved directly from the impulse to the action. He had naught more than his bare hands wherewith to shatter the glittering stone, and he knew that he could beat against that dazzling cliff of light for ages to come without dislodging a single shining atom of crystal from that impervious surface. Therefore, he sought a tool.

Naught met his eye as he gazed impatiently around him. Naught, save for the mighty ring of standing stones. But at that sight he smiled, and his keen eye measured distances, hoping the stones were real enough to splinter the jewel, and not mere illusions.

He set his back against one great stone of the ring and heaved. It was like pushing against a marble mountain. For one man to dislodge this towering slab of flinty stone seemed impossible. It seemed so foolish to even contemplate that most men would not even have tried. He looked up at the soaring wall of the stone. It towered into the heavens thrice his own not inconsiderable height. And, from the immovable appearance of the monolith, it was buried deeper than one might guess into the nameless substance of the land. Yes, truly *impossible* . . .

Most men would not have even tried, I say. Aye, but Thongor was his own man, unique among the swarming millions of his fellows. A rare and strange being was this barbarian, a hero, a king, and such as he achieve the impossible by never shrinking back from attempting it.

He set one burly shoulder against the slab, and set his arms thus and so, and placed his feet, and drew deep a mighty breath, and heaved.

For a moment there was nothing. No movement. No slightest yielding. *Stop trying,* ghostly voices hammered in his brain. *It cannot be done,* they whined at him; *give up now—now—now!*

He strove on, muscles knotting with strain, face black with effort, mighty lungs panting, heart laboring.

Great thews swelled along massive shoulders and mighty arms, standing out hard and sharp-edged like worked bands of bronze. His feet dug down into the sandy soil. His hands clasped the edges of the huge slab, locked in place, and strained, knuckles whitening with effort.

The slab shuddered. It *gave,* slowly, slowly, earth buckling before it as the stone yielded inch by agonizing inch before the irresistible surge of Thongor's mighty thews.

As it began to topple, he released the stone and sprang back so as not to be caught as the buried portion came crashing up out of the sand. He stood panting, sucking air deep into his lungs, watching.

The seventh stone of the ring came thundering down and caught the jewel square. It cracked, a web of black lines slithering across the glittering surface from top to bottom. Thongor stood grinning, wondering what kind of eerie world this was, where spirit aches from effort as much as flesh ever did, where insubstantial lungs suck in unreal air, where an immaterial heart pounds against soul-ribs—*mad, nightmarish world!*

With a thunderous explosion, the titanic jewel shattered apart. Light blossomed in a flare of supernal brilliance, searing Thongor's eyes as with a lightning-flash. Utter flame sheeted up in a pyre of white fury. He felt the lash of light across his chest like the breath of an open furnace. The ground shuddered and recoiled, jumping underfoot.

Whatever terrific forces had been locked within the weird crystal, held in precarious balance by enormous strictures, they reacted with incredible violence once the glassy prison-wall was breached.

He opened his eyes. The fallen stone was gone. The crystal had vanished, leaving a monstrous pit of smoking earth. One by one—dislodged, perchance, by the blast or the erupting gem, or falling now that their purpose was lost—the six remained stones of the ring fell, collapsing like a house of cards. The impact of their fall made the plain shiver.

The sword was gone!

No, there it was—a vagrant gleam of steely light flashed mirror-bright within the smoking shadow of the pit. He scrambled down into it, earth sliding treacherously underfoot, the strange dry smell of burnt earth thick and hot in his nostrils. He clasped the glittering pommel and dragged the shining sword up out of a light covering of fallen dirt. He lifted the blade up into the air and watched it catch the light and flash with incredible brilliance, feeling deep satisfaction within him. Now, with a sword in his hand, he felt somehow complete.

Then the sword was gone—utterly! Only the cross-shaped hilt of red gold remained in his hand. He blinked and looked again, eyes narrowing with disbelief. But it was so—he had felt the colossal weight of the great sword when he raised it high above his head—then his flesh was tingling with weird awe as he felt the burden of its massive weight inexplicably lighten in his very grasp!

Brows knotted, he bent a perplexed gaze on the useless swordhilt in his hands.

What was that? That flicker of light, like a dim ray of brilliance probing up from the flat cross-hilt? For a moment he had thought he saw a thin, insubstantial beam of white light thrusting up from the hilt, a beam *seven feet long*.

Now it was gone again. But, in the brief moment that he saw the enigmatic light-ray, he felt a tingle of awesome power run through him, and his flesh shuddered with a surge of strength and vitality. . . .

He stood for a long, long time, hefting the T-shaped piece of heavy gold thoughtfully.

All is illusion, nothing is quite what it seems . . .

Everything in this dark realm of Avangra the Death-Lord is but the analogue of its earthly self . . . even your own body.

He hefted the hilt with knotted brow, then he grinned and came up out of the pit, still holding the pommel.

Perhaps this Sword of Light was a test of some kind. The thought touched his mind in a vagrant wisp of thought: *is this great blade the Shadowland analogue of mine own great Valkarthan broadsword?*

He did not know the answer to any of these questions. All in this dim nightmare realm was a mockery, a clash of echoes, a vague and haunting mass of intertwining symbols. But he would bear the swordhilt with him, in any case. Perhaps he was a fool to burden himself with so seemingly useless an object, and perhaps not. At any rate, he would see.

He went forward towards the shadowy horizon across the ghostly plain. And the proof of the sword came upon him far sooner than he had ever dreamed it might, for suddenly—out of nothingness and night, a vast black shape rose up from the plain before him—a huge, hulking, shaggy ogre-like form with blazing eyes and frigid breath that blew across his flesh like a blast of wintry wind.

And there in the Land of Shadows beyond the Gates of Life and the dark Portals of the Tomb, Thongor of Valkarth found himself locked in uncanny battle with a thing he could neither see nor feel—but that held him in a grip like Death itself!

Chapter 7: THE ROAD OF MILLIONS OF YEARS

His great blade cleaves through empty air,
It flays his flesh with icy breath.
How fight a Thing that is not there,
Or kill, when all this land is Death?

—*Thongor's Saga,* Stave XVIII

Without an instant's warning, the swordsman of Valkarth found himself fighting for his very life!

A mammoth claw seized him about his lean waist with crushing force. A tidal wave of blackness rose before him, blotting out the light. He swung balled fists that hissed through thin air—*through* the black shape that had nearly engulfed him. The blackness clung and crushed him, but his blows met no opposition whatsoever . . . it was like striking out against a formless shadow!

In the viselike grip of the Blackness, in the whirling confusion of the fight, Thongor found it impossible to gain any clear impression of his weird adversary. He had a blurred, swift glimpse of looming darkness, or a vast, heaving, shaggy form, thick-set and stump-legged, with sloping shoulders and bestial paws—one of which closed crushingly around his lean midsection—but little else.

A flashing glimpse of great blazing eyes like moons of

cold fire in a broad, blunt bull-like head thatched with thick black shag. Then a start of pure horror went through him like a blade of ice as *another* head lifted into view!

The shambling thing shuffled thick legs. The massive paw about his waist tightened—lifted. The shaggy twin heads glared at him. Fanged maws gaped wide—and his flesh thrilled to the incredible blast of superarctic cold that breathed from the black jaws of the two-headed ogre.

The icy blast of its breath was unendurable. The warrior could feel granules of ice form on his panting chest and swinging arms. His senses blurred, his heart labored.

What use was it to fight? Better to let go, to slide down into the soft blackness, to give up, yield, surrender . . . why fight on against that which you could not defeat?

The insidious thoughts whispered through his dazed mind. For a moment—for a long, breathless, terrible moment he felt the dragging pull of the temptation and felt himself hover on the brink of yielding to the seductive urge. But then his manhood reasserted itself. From some inward source, fury came boiling up within him. He had fought men and beasts, demons and Gods ere now—and never had he surrendered!

He swung another enfeebled blow with the useless gold swordhilt he clasped in one weakening hand—and even as the grim refusal to yield welled up within him, a strange force awoke—

The Sword of Light blazed up!

Fourth from the T-shaped hilt a beam of blinding white radiance flamed—a searing ray of utter brightness seven feet long flashed into being! It was as if his very determination *not* to yield had somehow triggered into existence the enchanted blade.

In his wild swing, the blade sank deep in the boulderlike chest of the Black One. The misty stuff from which the ogre's body was wrought—insubstantial to his own fists—yielded terribly to the flashing blade of light. A vast slab of cloudy substance was hewn away. It went floating off to the left, out of the range of Thongor's vision, and as it drifted away the smoky substance was crumbling into thin vapor.

The ogre howled soundlessly. The chill blast of its breath swept him from head to foot. But a tingling surge of warmth traveled down his arm from the blazing sword and he felt his cold flesh thaw as the current ran through him. Ice-dust vanished from his chest.

He swung the Sword of Light, slashing completely through the wrist of the paw that clasped him. It came apart, breaking up in a seething mass of roiling vapors, and he dropped to the desert plain, grinning. Now the tide of battle was on his side!

He waded in, swinging the magic blade lustily. The shaggy ogre stumbled back from his slashing assault.

Within moments he had slain, or dispersed, the monster and it was naught but a cloud of slowly expanding mist. He stood watching the vapors evaporate, feeling the lusty pride of victory. The sword had become once again naught but a useless pommel of red gold.

Now he was beginning to learn something of the strange laws that governed this peculiar astral realm where nothing was what it seemed and each thing was the analogue—the reflection, echo, or shadow—of something else.

The moment he had conquered his own fear, he had begun to conquer the demon.

Had the demon been but the symbolic form of his fear?

Perhaps. He could not be certain. But he recalled the earlier incident when, at first, the task of freeing the sword from the jewel had seeming imposing, if not impossible. The moment he had determined it *could* be done, he did it!

Thongor shrugged away such baffling thoughts. His way was the raw red road of direct and primal action. These musings were suited to philosophers or fools—or both.

He strode forward, the swordhilt clasped in his hand.

He walked now upon a broad and level road of dressed stone.

It had emerged out of the colorless sands of the desert plain by such gradual stages as to be imperceptible. But now the road had fully risen above the drifting sands, so he let it be his guide.

Straight as an arrow's flight it ran from this place to the

dim and distant horizon. The horizon was clouded and veiled from his sight so he could not make out towards what goal he strove. He went forward, uncaring.

It occurred to the Valkarthan to wonder who had set this road here, and for what reason.

To this question no answer seemed possible. He wondered of what earthly journey or state the road was the analogue.

As he went forward, he began to glimpse curious shapes set up along the road at intervals. They did not so much appear out of nothingness as it was he who gradually became aware of their being. After a time he could see them clearly. And they, more than anything else he had yet encountered in this weird spirit realm, seemed truly symbolic.

Thrones of odd and antique design rose to either side of the stone-paved way. They were gray with dust, cloaked in cobwebs, riven and gnawed with time.

Heaps of crowns and coronets, stacks of scepters and rods of kingly power, were bundled together with tattered rags of velvet and satin and ermine, the moldy remnants of royal robes of state.

Here and there like crumbling monuments rose the shattered gates of cities unknown to him, and the decayed porticos of vast palaces. Busts and statues of forgotten kings stood on cracked pedestals, or lay fallen in the dust.

And there were ruined flags and standards and all manner of proud regal banners, withering into dust. Some were bravely wrought of gold and silver wire on fine silks and some were woven through and through with glittering gems, and some were of humbler stuff, but all were crumbling and decaying before the breath of time.

As he strode along the way, he puzzled as to the meaning of these broken and dust-shrouded remains of royal glory. The road passed them by as if it were the mighty and all-encompassing River of Time itself, which passeth and leaveth behind to molder lost and forgotten the thrones and empires of past glory. He brooded somberly on this thought, that be they never so strong-founded, so rich in fame and conquest and majesty, every great realm and nation of man shall fall and founder at last, for none be so secure that Time the Conqueror can not bring them low into the humble dust.

He never knew how many hours or days the journey took, for here in this dim land of perpetual and unchanging twilight time passed unheralded and unnoticed—if, indeed, time existed at all.

Perhaps his journey took but instants, perhaps aeons—but he felt nothing of bodily fatigue. His bare feet trampled the stone-build Road of the Millions of Years (as he came in time to think of it) but the astral stuff of which this ghostly simulacrum of his earthly form was composed seemed insensible to all fatigue. Or perhaps his journey was *itself* an illusion of his dreaming brain. He never knew
. . . .

Now and then beside the road he glimpsed in the eerie half-light the withered corpses or gaunt mummies of ancient, long-dead kings. Some slept in broken tombs of snowy marble. Some were laid to rest in gilded coffins worked all over with hieroglyphic texts. Yet others sat stiff and dry on their thrones with tarnished crowns set upon their brown leathery brows.

He saw as well that gods can die in the fullness of eternal time. For here and there in the symbolic ruins that lined the sides of the vast avenue down which he journeyed to the unknown horizon he came upon the crude totems and rough-hewn idols of fallen and forgotten gods whose very names, perchance, had faded into the mists of legend, as had their worshippers.

What hope for men, he thought with grim humor, *when even gods may die?*

Then it was that he came upon the first obstacle that he had met since the Phantom of Fear had challenged him hours or ages ago. As he stopped short and stared at the impassable barrier he felt again the hopelessness of his position rise to overwhelm him—the bodiless wraith of a dead man, lost and wandering in the strange half-worlds of this mystic Borderland between the worlds!

He looked at the River of Fire and knew he could not pass it.

Chapter 8: RIVER OF FIRE, WALL OF ICE

> Like molten flame the waters glide
> Across his path to block his way;
> He does not shrink nor turn aside,
> But fights the floods as best he may.

—*Thongor's Saga,* Stave XVIII

A broad river of crimson flame cut across his way, stretching from horizon to horizon. It sprang into being between one step and the next, and now as he halted short upon the very brink of the blazing flood he saw that a single unwary step might have pitched him to a terrible death in the fiery embrace of the liquid flames.

He stepped back and looked upon the incredible barrier.

Whatever the waters of the river were fashioned of, they burned with a seething fury. In the long annals of his earthly wanderings and adventures, Thongor of Valkarth had seen streams of blazing lava no more fiery than this strange flood of burning fluid that now blocked his path. But the lava had been molten rock, a thick and viscous substance like mud, heated to a cheery cherry-red glow, its wrinkled and sluggish surface crawling with flickering yellow flames. This was different—the magic river was a broad and ponderous flood of what appeared to be water—but water that blazed with great shaking banners of gold and orange and crimson flames that shot ten paces into the air. And the light shed by the burning water was so fierce and intolerable that he must shield his eyes with a lifted hand or be blinded.

As best he might, half-blinded by the glare, he measured the width of the tide. Perhaps, he hoped, it would prove narrow enough so that he might cross it with a mighty leap. No. The burning river was thirty yards across.

He looked about him in the grip of growing helplessness. It seemed impossible that he could go around the river of fire, for it stretched straight as a boundary-line from horizon to horizon. Or so, he reminded himself, it *seemed*—for he had learned by now that in this Empire of Death one could not trust eyesight alone.

His next thought was to consider dislodging one of the huge paving-stones whereof the road was composed, so as to make a mighty raft. Thongor knew that a flat stone will float for a time upon the surface of molten lava. He wondered if such were also the case with this river of flaming water.

He pried loose a small slab of stone from the borders of the road and heaved it into the fiery gulf—only to see it sink on the instant without a trace in the flaming waves.

That slim chance seemed to exhaust the store of possibilities—at least for the moment. How, then, was he to cross the blazing barrier? Or was his strange quest to end here on the blistering brink of the magic stream? What else was there for him to do, but to turn back at this point?

He stood staring thoughtfully at the surface of the road, where it broke off abruptly before the blazing torrent. The ancient stones were shaken and dislodged and dry weeds grew here and there between them, even upon the very edge of the flood of crimson flame——

He froze with astonishment.

Was his strange quest to end here on the blistering edge of the enchanted barrier?

A grim smile broke the masklike impassivity of his features. He burst into laughter. Would he never learn to distrust the evidence of his senses in this ghostly realm? He had become so accustomed by now to the fact that this astral counterpart of his earthly body was largely insensitive to fatigue and the ills of mortality, that he had not until this very moment noticed that the river of fire cast fierce red light—but shed no heat!

For there, on the very verge and margin of the flaming stream, dry dead weeds grew up between the paving stones—weeds that should by all the laws of nature have shriveled and burst into flame from such near proximity to the burning waters—if those burning waters were *real*.

He flung himself prone beside the river and, greatly daring, thrust his hand into the seething flames.

To vision alone, it was a terrible sight. His bare flesh vanished in the crimson smoky light as leaping tongues of flame coiled about his hand, but he felt *nothing*.

The river of fire was mere illusion, and naught more!

He stepped into the roaring flood and stood there. The racing tide came to his chest. The shaking banners of crimson flame towered far over his head. The light was so fierce that he was forced to close his eyes against the glare.

But he felt nothing at all. No heat, no tugging current. Nothing.

Laughing with grim humor, he strode across the river and as soon as it lay behind him it vanished completely in an instant, ceasing to exist as swiftly as it had flashed into being. Behind him stretched an unbroken surface of the Road and nothing more. Smiling, he strode forward.

It was not long before yet another barrier opposed his way.

He strode into a thickening fog whose gray vapor rose boiling up from the surface of the land and condensed before him—suddenly clearing away.

A vast wall of glittering ice marched like a range of glass mountains across the world before him from horizon to horizon. It rose in a sheer cliff, breaking into a sparkling mass of crystal pinnacles at its cloven crest. Dim light flickered and twinkled from the glistening facets of the wall.

Thongor faced it, wondering if this was naught but another illusion. He felt no dank breath of cold from the icy mass—and from his boyhood in the frozen Northlands of the Lemurian continent, he recalled the chilling fog that blew numbingly from the massive glaciers of that boreal realm.

If the wall of ice were no illusion, but reality, then his quest had reached his end. He knew of no way wherewith he could scale the sheer and glistening cliff. It towered fifty paces above the stone-paved surface of the road, its distant peaks and planes sparkling dimly above in the mystic twilight, catching vagrant gleams from some unknown source of light unseen above.

He strode up to the icy surface and thrust his hand against it.

His hand sank effortlessly in the glassy blue surface.

He felt no obstruction, no cold. This, too, was but a mirage sensible to his vision only.

Thongor strode forward into the chill embrace of the ice, and his bare flesh crawled in anticipation of the wet cold —but he felt it not. Instead, he found that he could penetrate the sheer face of the glistening cliff. He was now *inside* the wall of ice!

It was an unforgettable experience. As far as the eye could tell, he was frozen deep within the mighty glacier. From within a dim blue vista stretched away to all sides. Fractured planes and facets, the internal structure of the ice, bent and twisted the light. He was alone in a weird world, bathed in dim blue luminance.

He strode on, passing through fantastic crystal caverns and past dangling stalactites like mighty spears of glass and through solid inner walls of ice where his own distorted reflection strode toward him and through which he passed. Strange and terrible was the beauty of this crystal world to the sight, yet when he closed his eyes it was as if he strode through utterly empty air.

What had he learned thus far along the road? That when he conquered his own fear, the two-headed ogre fell away before him into nothingness? That when he refused to be daunted by seemingly impassable obstacles and pressed forward against them, they proved to be not impassable at all? That the mere fact of *striving* to accomplish that which seemed overwhelming, was the key to all accomplishment?

Perhaps. He was to remember these strange incidents long, and to ponder over these symbolic teachings from the gods.

The icy ramparts vanished behind him once he had

emerged beyond the wall. Looking back, he could see naught but the level surface of the road which extended to the dim mists of the horizon behind him.

He turned and looked ahead. Now he was very near to his goal—and still he did not know what the goal of this dreamlike journey was to be. But ahead of him there, where a mighty mass of mountains rose on the very edge of this nightmarish world, the road ended at last. He continued his journey towards the mountains.

It seemed impossible that he had nearly reached the mountains. He remembered, at the beginning of the journey, glimpsing them at the far distant edge of the world. Somehow, in this timeless half-world beyond Time, he had traversed an inconceivable distance—the full breadth of this world—and soon he stood before the titanic mountains which lifted sheer from the flat surface of the plain to tower above him against the twilit sky.

The mountains were no illusion, as a touch proved! They rose, a mass of dark rock grown together, forming an enormous cuplike depression far over his head, with a higher wall of cliffs beyond the cup-shaped mesa. It was like a stupendous throne, he thought, for the massive mountains seemed to form into a chair of stone whose proportions were virtually unthinkable.

And then, as he stood before the Throne of Mountains, staring up, he saw a great shadow take shape and substance out of the dim nothingness here at the very edge of this world.

Manlike it was, cloudy and vague of outline. Two towering pillars formed its legs, swathed in the folds of cloud like some misty robe. Far, far above he could make out the colossal proportions of its vast chest and shoulders and mighty face.

The visage that stared down at him from the heights was not unlike the face of a mortal man . . . a man old and wise and kingly, with the shadowy cataract of a majestic beard tumbling down the titanic vista of its chest. Keen eyes, piercing as stars, blazed down at him and the cloudy cowl of those dim robes shadowed the mighty head.

Against its chest, the misty figure clasped a titanic book

sealed with seven locks. One great hand lay across this book, and each finger of that hand was greater in girth and longer in length than Thongor's body.

He knew that tome for the Book of Millions of Years, wherein (sayeth legend) are writ the annals of all time . . . time past and time present and time unborn.

And by the book, by the attribute of its very form, he knew the phantom being above him for Pnoth the Lord of Starry Wisdom.

A vast awe came over him. Humbled, the shade of Thongor bowed before the misty figure on its titanic mountain-throne.

He was in the living presence of a god.

The Third Book

SLAVES OF THE PIRATE EMPIRE

"Below the Gulf of Patanga, aye, where it mingles with the immeasurable waters of Yashengzeb Chun the Southern Sea, there stands a great promontory of rock whereon is builded Tarakus the Pirate City, a lawless and bloody realm that knoweth no rule save the lust of gold. Therefrom, in the long years ahead, a peril shall rise up to enshadow the Cities of the West, so beware, O Thongor . . . take warning and beware."

—*The Great Book of Sharajsha the Wizard of Lemuria*

Chapter 9: ABOVE THE CLOUDS

> Forth from the stronghold of their foes
> They fled into the black of night,
> But from the gloom new perils rose
> To bar their freedom and their flight.

> —*Thongor's Saga,* Stave XVIII

Charn Thovis and Prince Thar flung themselves out of the palace window into the empty night. Blackness closed about them. They floated above the towers in the grip of mighty winds that whistled around them, tugging at their cloaks and blowing their hair behind them.

The skybelts were new and scarcely tested: a plain leathern harness plated with a thin sheath of urlium, the magic metal discovered years before by the old alchemist, Oolim Phon. While urlium resisted gravity and "fell up," the harness plates of the silvery alloy were not sufficient to render the warrior and the young boy fully weightless. Iothondus of Kathool, the wise young Nephelos whose science-magic had created powerful new weapons for the warriors of Patanga, had discovered a method which multiplied the lifting power of the magic metal.

The secret lay in the use of sithurls, the weird power crystals found only on the trackless plains of the mysterious East where the Blue Nomads of the Five Hordes roamed and warred against cruel beast and savage enemies. Sithurls absorbed the rays of the sun and transformed solar energy into electric force. The sithurl which adorned like a brooch the flying harness Charn Thovis wore was small but potent. At a touch it released a surge of curious force which charged the urlium plating, energizing the magic metal to many times its normal lifting power.

As Charn Thovis hurtled through the night, he strove to wring every erg of antigravitic force from the energized harness. The crystals were not inexhaustible. His flight into the palace had drained much of the power stored within the strange green crystal. Now, as he felt the pull of the earth below, despair gnawed at him. He knew the small power-charge of the sithurl was not strong enough to sustain the double weight of the boy and himself for long.

Unless he could think of some haven or conceive of some plan, the crystal's waning strength would give out and they would float down to earth in the very streets which were now swarming with the patrols of Dalendus Vool.

Twisting in mid-flight, Charn Thovis came to rest on a high balcony that jutted from a building near the palace. He paused there, searching his wits for some mode of escape. He had not contemplated the need to carry the prince to safety when making his plans. His discovery of the drugged and entranced Sarkaja had thrown all his plans awry.

"What's wrong, Charn Thovis?" Thar demanded.

"Nothing. The skybelt does not have enough power to lift us out of the city," he said. He had explained just enough of their peril for the boy to grasp the dilemma they were in.

Thar looked about him at the nighted city and the moon-less sky of turgid vapors above. He was delighted with the novelty of the experience, and felt no fear of danger—it was all a thrilling adventure to him. It was, in fact, his *first* adventure, and he was enjoying it hugely!

He looked up, tossing back his unshorn mane of black hair.

"Then let's take an airboat," he suggested, reasonably enough. "There's a landing stage on the roof of this build-ing."

Charn Thovis looked at the lad with some surprise. Of course the prince did not fully comprehend the depth of their difficulties—how explain to the boy that the armed forces of his city had been subverted to the will of his foe, Dalendus Vool, or that he could no longer even trust the commanders of his father's fighting men? But he had expected the youth to be more of a burden than an active cool-headed and intelligent comrade. He grinned. He should have guessed he could hope for more, for was this not the son of Thongor the Mighty?

"Good idea. At least, it's worth a try," he said. "Come, up on my shoulders again and hold tight. I hope there's enough power in the belt to lift us to the rooftop!"

He sprang again into the dark womb of night and felt the winds around their flying forms like great wings beating. Prince Thar laughed with joy at the thrill of flight but Charn Thovis was grimly measuring the pace of their ascent against the height of the roof still far above their level.

The green and silver fires of the belt's sithurl burnt low and flickered feebly. With each wavering flicker he felt the lifting force of the belt weaken, although he did not call the boy's attention to this and hoped the youth did not notice.

Then the sithurl's force died and they fell . . . but slowly. The urlium plating over the harness still allayed the drag of their weight, but no longer was its lifting power sufficient to render them completely weightless. They would float down to the street far below, unless . . .

He reached out desperately and seized a grinning stone face as he floated down past it. His sweating fingers slipped over the smooth marble of the carven monster's beak— then caught and clung to the fanged and open mouth. For a time they hung floating to and fro in the shifting wind and Charn Thovis thanked the gods that the innate lifting power of the magic metal harness sustained the greater part of their weight. It did not also occur to him to render up thanks to the ancient architect who had adorned the upper terraces of this mansion with the protruding stone gargoyle heads.

Now he must climb up the face of the building, hand over hand, in almost total darkness. Wind howled about him, whipping the boy's shaggy mane in his eyes. Luckily, the façade of the building was thick with carven ornament which afforded a variety of handholds. Still, his arms were sore and aching with strain by the time he hauled the boy and himself over the lip of the roof and could rest on level ground.

But there was no time to rest, to catch his breath. A great airboat was before them, floating free on its anchorcable above the landing stages. And a warrior in the silver gilt harness and blue cloak of the Air Guard came forward to demand their names and their reason for being here—at sword's point.

He carried one of the new sithurl lamps and lifted it, sending a shaft of bright illumination to bathe the two fugitives. Then he paused, gaping with surprise, when he saw and recognized the boy's face.

"My Prince? What——"

Charn Thovis sprang like a great black vandar of the jungles upon his back and pulled him down, clubbing him into insensibility with a powerful blow of his fist. Then, as the boy turned to him in surprise, he snatched his hand and gestured towards the flying boat.

"Swiftly now, no time for questions. We must be off at once. Even now the guards of Dalendus Vool may have noticed your absence from the palace and the alarm may sound at any moment——"

"But Charn Thovis, you struck him!" the boy protested.

He gripped the boy's shoulders and looked into his face.

"My Prince, look at me! Trust me! I know all this is strange to you and that you have many questions, but *trust* me," he said urgently. "At the Hills of the Thunder-Crystals, I saved the life of your father and my Lord. Believe me, Thar, I serve him no less loyally at this moment!"

Thar stared at him, eyes wide and wondering. Then something of Thongor's grimness came into his eyes, filling them with the steel of determination.

"Lead, Charn Thovis, and I follow. I will trust you," he said slowly.

There was no time for thanks. He wrung the youth's hand in silence, then assisted him to clamber up the rope ladder to the rear deck of the airboat which pitched and wobbled under their weight. Once in the cabin he triggered

the motors into action and bade Thar cast off the mooring
lines. In an instant they floated free, drifting on the wind.
Then the keen blades of the rotors bit into the nightwind
and they were off, rising above the great city in a vast
ascending spiral.

This was one of the newest models, with many times the
speed of the older craft. Iothondus of Kathool had perfected a sithurl engine to drive the whirling blades, replacing the old spring-driven rotors of old. The craft responded
superbly to Charn Thovis' light touch on the controls. It
rose like an eagle floating on the wind.

They ascended to the twenty-thousand-foot level.
Patanga was far below them now and they could dimly
make out the great central plaza and the broad avenue of
the Thorian Way stretching across the city to the mighty
wall of flame-colored stone. Dim light twinkled on the gliding surfaces of the Twin Rivers and from this height they
could see ships moored at the long stone quays. They
looked like toy galleys at this height.

He had not really expected they could fly from the city
unchallenged. The keen eyes of the Air Guard patrolled
these skies and as their airboat hovered above the night-
black city, patrol boats darted towards them.

"Look!" Thar cried, pointing through the forward windows. "The patrol has seen us!"

"Hang on, my Prince," Charn Thovis said grimly.
"Perhaps we can outdistance them."

He had intended to strike north for the stronghold of the
Lord Mael. But now he must find a different route, for it
would never do to lead the enemy straight to their goal. So
instead he headed west, out over the dim waters of the
great gulf that cleft the continent like a mighty wedge of
water from Tarakus on the coast to the very quays of
Patanga.

The rotors snarled a harsh song of power as they drove
the floater through the night skies like a silver arrow. Wind
whistled about the sleek lines of their glittering urlium hull.
Charn Thovis, seated at the controls, aimed the needle
prow of the airboat due west and they hurtled into the
darkness.

"They are still following us, Charn Thovis," the boy observed calmly. "There are two of them, armed with lightning guns."

"Courage, my Prince. Perhaps we can lose them in the clouds," he said, turning the craft south over the wide waters. Some leagues south he spied a dense cloudbank and drove toward it with every erg of power he could coax or command from the laboring engines. It was no good, however. Like hunting hounds, the two patrol boats clung on their trail.

The pursuers and the pursued were evenly matched. Their vessels were of equal speed and size. However, Charn Thovis had a slight edge on those who followed him. They were two-man ships, weighed down with two fully-armed warriors, whereas his craft was somewhat lighter in burthen, since he had only the boy with him. And he had a few seconds' head start. He milked these slim advantages for all they were worth.

Now signal flags broke from the prows of the pursuit craft, colors streaming in the winds.

" 'Surrender or be shot down,' " the boy read their code in a grave voice. "Why would they shoot us down, Charn Thovis? We have done no wrong."

"They think we have, my Prince. The alarm must have sounded by now, surely. They think I have kidnapped you!" he replied tensely.

"Then, since they know that I am aboard, surely they will not dare to fire upon us," the boy reasoned. "They are bluffing!"

The warrior smiled. The boy had courage and a clear head, and he kept his wits about him even in direst danger. How proud Thongor would be if he could see his son in this hour!

"Perhaps you are right. Let us hope so, at any rate."

For nearly half an hour the airboat fled south, trailed by its two pursuers. It would seem that Prince Thar had guessed correctly that the patrol craft would not dare fire upon the airboat containing the prince. At least, the lightning guns remained silent. But the patrol ships still hurtled after them, neither gaining nor losing. And with every passing instant Charn Thovis felt less confident that he could shake off pursuit in the dense cloudbank that loomed ahead. For now the vapors above had parted and the great golden moon of old Lemuria shone through, filling the night with its serene and brilliant light. The mild waters of the gulf below were transformed into a vast blazing shield. In the clear moonlight, the urlium hull glittered brightly, and Charn Thovis feared that even amidst the heavy clouds his pursuers would be able to spot his craft without great difficulty.

Now he was in the cloudbank. He turned the prow from due south and, under cover of the roiling mists, angled his flight to the southeast towards the city of Zangabal on the far shore. If he could elude his pursuers he and the lad might find refuge in that friendly city, now a member of the Empire, for the Sark's brother, Prince Zuel, had been one of the loyalists who had met with Mael and Charn Thovis at Sardath Keep.

But *could* he shake off pursuit?

He looked behind him but could see neither of the pursuing craft through the seething mists.

"Hang on, my Prince!" he called out. "I am going to drop down to the ten-thousand-foot level. Perhaps they will continue searching for us above."

He cut the power and let the airboat slide down through the fogs. This was somewhat dangerous, he knew. Perhaps the cloudbanks did not extend below ten thousand feet. In that case, they would lose the cover of the clouds and be clearly visible to the patrol ships if either of them ventured down to a lower level. It was a risk, but a calculated one, and Charn Thovis believed it wise to dare it.

Even as he had feared they broke free of the clouds at ten thousand feet and skimmed along through open air, clearly silhouetted against the bright waters of the gulf which mirrored the great full moon.

He bent the prow towards the distant spires of Zangabal and prayed for the moon to again vanish behind the dense mists that had obscured her golden face through the earlier hours of the night. Instead, everything began to go wrong at once.

"Charn Thovis—*look!*"

The boy's sharp outcry caught his attention. And he turned to see the patrol ships breaking out of the clouds far above and behind him. And then he turned forward again to see a danger even more terrible.

The airboats of Patanga were not unchallenged in their supremacy over the skies. For the great pterodactyls—the monster flying reptiles of the steaming fens of the lost Jurassic Era—still survived here in southern and tropic Lemuria to haunt the heavens. *Lizard-hawks,* the Patanganya called the dread and dragonlike predators of the skies.

And there, outlined like monster bats against the golden face of the moon, two great lizard-hawks hung like black demons from some hellish nightmare.

Even as Charn Thovis saw them with a thrill of cold fear, they folded their mighty bat-wings and fell towards him, cruel breaks gaping wide with the lust to kill!

Chapter 10: IN THE DRAGONS' GRIP

Black wings thunder and fanged jaws gape
As the lizard-hawks fall on their flying prey!
From the dragon's claws there is no escape,
Above the waters at break of day . . .

—*Thongor's Saga,* Stave XVIII

Changan Jal was the senior Otar in command of the two patrol craft that had chased the airboat wherein Charn Thovis and young Prince Thar fled from Patanga. Only seconds before his pilot spied the unauthorized ascent of the stolen floater from the rooftop landing stage above the mansion near the palace, he had read the alarm flags which burst from the spire of the Air Citadel near the center of the city—flags which warned of the escape of a renegade Black Dragon who had daringly kidnapped the nine-year-old prince from his palace suite.

No agent of Dalendus Vool was Otar Changan Jal, but a loyal warrior of Patanga who had gained great honors in the service of Thongor the Mighty. But so cunningly had Dalendus Vool assumed power over the City of the Flame that even those loyal to Thongor were not aware that treachery held the royal throne and the reins of military command. Hence, as might any loyal Patangan warrior, he had bent every effort to apprehend the renegade Charn Thovis.

Grimly had he clung to the trail of the stolen airboat, following it many leagues south over the waters of the broad gulf. Through the seething clouds he had searched for the fleeing traitor and the helpless prince, whom he imagined to be bound and captive in the hands of the traitor.

Now his heart leaped with grim joy as he spotted the silvery dart of the airboat far below his height—only to have the cold breath of dread chill his joy a moment later when he saw the assault of the flying dragons!

Breathless, Changan Jal and his pilot watched as the small craft below circled to elude the hurtling lizard-hawks. Black bat-wings spread suddenly to break their descent and the reptiles uttered hissing screams of rage as their helpless prey fled from the crushing grip of their talons.

Full-grown were these two Terrors of the Skies. Forty feet from tip to tip measured the mighty expanse of their wings. The great claws which armed their feet were enough to tear through stone walls or to crumple sheets of metal. In the grip of the flying dragons even the powerful flying ships of Patanga were helpless, unless—

"Use your lightning gun, you fool!" Changan Jal hissed between clenched teeth as he helplessly watched the floater circling and weaving desperately, seeking to evade the clutching claws of the furious reptiles.

Even as he watched, Charn Thovis triggered the weapon mounted on his needle-prow. Dim night brightened dazzlingly as the sithurl weapon spoke. A spear of intolerable white fire flashed from the darting craft to catch one circling lizard-hawk squarely in his underbelly.

Caught in the ravening fury of the energy beam, the dragon of the skies was torn apart. The fire-bolt clove through his mailed girth and ripped his body asunder. Fragments of the slain pterodactyl fluttered to the surface of the gulf far below, wrapped in flames.

The second sky monster circled a moment—then struck. He fell upon the craft with outstretched claws, like some titanic hawk. The airboat shuddered from stem to stern with the impact of the collision. Powerful claws tightened on the needle prow and bright metal crumpled like torn paper. As the circling patrol boats far above watched breathlessly, unable to help, the weight of the lizard-hawk crushed down the nose of the flying vessel. Then it struck at the cabin with its cruel hooked beak. Glass splintered and metal struts gave way before the ferocity of the assault.

As the crippled airboat sank under the monster's weight toward the gliding waves far below, the sky dragon struck again and again—great battering blows with that powerful beak, shattering blows like some enormous pile-driver or battering-ram. Blows that stove in the hull and crumpled the decks of the flying boat.

There was nothing the two Patangan patrol craft could do to help, so swiftly had the flying monsters struck, so great had been the distance between the fleeing vessel and their own boats.

So Changan Jal and his pilot watched helplessly as the pterodactyl literally tore the airboat apart. Sparkling fragments of the urlium plating, torn away like tin foil from the structure of steel, went floating upwards into the heavens as their lifting powers, no longer borne down to perfect balance by the counterweight of the steel framework, carried them high into the air where the first beams of dawn were touching the high-piled clouds to flame.

The framework of steel beams, ripped apart by the tear-ing claws, fell into the gulf below. Voicing a shattering scream of victory, the sky dragon circled once and flew away.

Of the stolen airboat wherein Prince Thar and Charn Thovis had made their escape from the City of the Flame, there was no sign left. It had been utterly destroyed.

Of the prince and his captor there also remained no sign. With a heavy heart, Changan Jal was forced to the conclusion that the lizard-hawk had slain and devoured both the heir to the throne of Patanga and the renegade Black Dragon warrior who had, for some unknown reason, abducted him.

The pilot of the patrol boat turned a tense white face on his grim-jawed commander. "What shall we do now, sir?"

The Otar shook his head sadly. "I fear there is little we *can* do," he admitted. "I would order us down to the surface of the gulf to search for wreckage, but what would be the use of that? Even if Charn Thovis and Prince Thar escaped being devoured by the lizard-hawk and fell from their ship when it was torn asunder, they could not by any stretch of the imagination have survived the fall into the gulf, for their ship was more than a mile aloft when attacked. No . . . I fear there is naught we can do here. Let us return to Patanga and make our report." His grim face tightened and his voice became dull, as he added, "I have served the House of Chond and the House of Valkarth for eleven years, first in the legions and now in the Air Guard, and never have I seen a darker hour than this, Anzan Varl. Alas, the Sarkaja—poor, sad Queen! First her lord the king taken from her, and now her only son! The news is harsh and pitiful, but we must bear it to the palace. Come, signal our companion ship and turn about to home."

In a few moments the two ships circled the area one more time, then dipping their prows in silent tribute to the fallen prince, they rose to the fifteen-thousand-foot level and flew off to the north where the stone walled city rose at the mouth of the Twin Rivers, bearing to the Patangan nation the sad news of the passing of Prince Thar, son of Thongor and last survivor of the ill-fated House of Valkarth.

The morning sun rose brilliantly over the edge of the world and flooded all the land with light. Clear and undimmed were his rays, for what knew the sun of the end of dynasties or the death of princes? They were all one to him in his lone splendor as he drenched the empire in dawn.

The news of Prince Thar's death came to Dalendus Vool and Mardanax of Zaar as they broke their morning fast on the terraces of the palace. Since assuming command of the empire as regent, Dalendus Vool had moved with all his entourage, among whom was the silent and hooded figure of Black Mardanax who rarely left the side of his tool, into sumptuous suites in the Palace of the Sarks.

When the word came to them, borne by a military equerry, the vapid Baron of Tallan trembled with terror and spilled the wine over his robes, lifting his querulous shrill voice in a babble of questions.

Mardanax swiftly assumed control of the scene, silencing the frightened Dalendus Vool with a cold phrase of stinging contempt, and bidding the captain withdraw and leave them.

"Oh, by all the gods, this is a judgment upon us, Master!" Dalendus Vool gasped, mopping his streaming brow and quivering jowls. "How can I rule now as regent, with the prince gone? Where is the legality of my claim? Will not the Lords Mael and Selverus demand I step down? What can we do——"

Mardanax surveyed the fat frightened noble with emerald eyes of icy disgust.

"Be silent, babbling fool, lest you alarm the servants," he commanded in a voice like iron. Whimpering and sobbing, Dalendus Vool gradually subsided.

"You are right in this, at any rate," the Black Druid said thoughtfully. "No longer can we rule Patanga in your name through the office of regent."

"Then let us make an end, Master, by all the gods! Let us go home to Tallan and make an end to all this——"

"I say again, fool, silence your tongue! Assume the outward form of manhood and courage, if inwardly you possess neither. No . . . your Regency ends here. Chaos

72

blast the child and that idiot of a hero who 'rescued' him! We would not have harmed the boy, just broken his mind and forced him to our bidding. As soon as it was safe to do so, Prince Thar could have abdicated in favor of yourself, then quietly died of a wasting fever, with no fuss. I abhor loose ends!"

Mardanax rubbed his jaw as his voice purred silkily.

"No, this overturns everything and breaks the careful web of all my plans. Now we must move swiftly to an alternate scheme. But I like it not. It is too sudden, too abrupt, and we have had no time to prepare for it, to lay the seeds in the minds of the court . . ."

"What—what alternate plan, O Master?" Dalendus Vool inquired doubtfully.

Mardanax smiled gently. "Why, you must marry the Princess Sumia, of course, and ascend the throne as true Sark of Patanga and Lord of the West," he purred.

The white-faced baron recoiled in astonishment. "I . . . marry . . . the Sarkaja?" he whimpered. "But how could I . . . why would she . . ."

The cold voice of the other broke ruthlessly through his babblings. "She will have no choice in the matter. My domination over her will is almost established. Soon, with further applications of the drug and further sessions of mental-probing, she will be totally subservient—even as art thou, O fat-faced fool! But it is too soon, too soon . . . I had not prepared for this exigency!"

"Are you certain it will—work?" the other protested feebly.

"In all candor—no, I am not certain. We have roused certain suspicions in the minds of the Sarkaja's closest friends by keeping them apart from her. This was needful, because my power over her will is not yet complete and I dare not display her before the people, least of all before her closest advisers, who will be certain to detect in her drugged, sonnambulistic manner that something is awry. Still, we have gained certain advantages. I can prolong the regency a little while by issuing a period of royal mourning under her seal and hand, suspending all councils and other acts of state for a few days in honor of the dead prince.

73

And, as well," he broke into a purring laugh, "we gain a very special advantage from this unexpected turn of events! Since the fool who abducted the boy was an officer of the Black Dragons, this gives us the perfect opportunity for placing Zad Komis, the commander of the regiment, in chains. We can claim there was a treasonous plot on the part of certain high officers in the command of Zad Komis to overthrow the throne and seize power. Excellent, excellent! We shall issue the order within the hour."

He broke off, chuckling, turning to look at the sad-faced baron who was staring into space with fear scrawled over his sagging visage.

"Come, my Lord Regent," Mardanax purred, "finish your breakfast and let us get to it. We have a busy morning ahead of us—declaring an official period of mourning and imprisoning the Daotar of the Black Dragons. As for your impending marriage, we shall issue that proclamation later in the week!"

Chapter 11: BARIM REDBEARD

The stars are bright, the wind is cold,
    The moon is drifting free.
We're out to seek for pirate gold
    Across a silver sea.

—*Sea Chantey of the Pirates of Tarakus*

There were voices shouting at him and a rocking movement that swung him back and forth. One arm was locked around something but he did not bother to open his eyes to see what it was. He had trouble breathing, so he opened his mouth and the next moment was spluttering and gagging, spitting out warm salt water. Then something splashed in the water near him and again he heard the voices yelling.

A moment later a brawny arm caught him around the throat and he heard a voice beside him telling him not to fight.

"No fight—float—let Thangmar hold you up," the voice said.

He relaxed, but still clung to the object which was now moving. He could hear it gagging and spitting up water and he opened his eyes and saw that it was the boy, Thar, whom he was holding. And he saw that the rocking motion he had been dimly aware of came from the waves, for the two of them were floating in the sea.

Then Thangmar, if that was his name, shouted for someone to throw him a rope and things went hazy for a while . . .

The next thing Charn Thovis knew he was lying on his back with a wooden deck under him, blinking sleepily up at a vast crimson sail in whose shadow he lay.

"Think he's comin' round," a gruff voice said.

"How about the young one?" another voice asked.

"He'll be fit enough, once we get all the water out of him," another voice said in the sing-song accent of Cadorna.

Charn Thovis levered himself up on one elbow and looked around. A circle of rough-looking men stood about him. Most were barefoot, though some wore long supple boots with flopping tops. Some were bare to the waist, long hair woven in thick braids down their backs; others wore bloused shirts of crimson silk with vests of black felt. Sashes of brightly patterned cloth were drawn tightly around their waists, and into these were thrust daggers with gold hilts. Leathern baldrics were slung across brawny, tanned chests and great swords slapped lean thighs. Broad-tipped scimitars of the East, or slim needle-sharp Tsargolian rapiers, for the most part, but he also saw notched cutlasses from the coastal cities and blunt *kunwars* of Chush and even some of the knob-headed, foot-long *tunga* throwing-sticks used by the savage tribes of jungle-clad Kovia.

They were men of many nations. Brown-skinned, black-haired Turanians such as himself, for the most part, but he saw more than a few slim Cadornyana with tawny golden skin and amber eyes among them, and even a giant Blue Nomad from the distant plains of the remote East. They wore gold rings and glittering gems in their earlobes. Some were marked with cutlass scars and others bore the skull brand that forever labeled them as outlaws. A few were bearded, which was rare among Turanians of Charn Thovis' race. They were a rough and savage lot, clad in tattered barbaric finery, but they seemed friendly enough and regarded Charn Thovis and Thar with eyes brightly curious and not seemingly hostile.

Indeed, one knelt down beside him with a steaming mug, put his brawny arm around Charn Thovis' shoulders to support him.

"Here, drink—soon you feel better!" he said in a coarse voice. The young warrior nodded gratefully and sipped the steaming brew—it was some kind of hot meat broth, laced with strong brandy, and tasted unspeakably delicious to one who had been drinking half the Gulf for the past three hours. He drank it slowly, feeling warmth spread through him and his mind grew clear.

When the lizard-hawk struck the floater, Charn Thovis had seized Thar and flung himself from the cabin into empty air. He still wore the skybelt, of course, and although its power crystal was drained of energy the urlium plating on the flying harness had enough lifting power to considerably lessen the speed of their fall.

Down through the dim air of early dawn they dropped slowly, the speed of their fall growing steadily, until they struck the briny waters of the Gulf of Patanga. Had not the flying harness reduced the weight of their bodies to a mere fraction, they could never have survived that endless fall. As it was, the impact drove them beneath the surging waves and struck young Thar unconscious. A strong swimmer, Charn Thovis dove and came up with the lad in his arms and held his face above the waves until he recovered his senses.

The two patrol craft had been too far above the stolen floater to help when it was attacked by the lizard-hawks.

Thus they were also too far away to see, among the falling wreckage torn from the hulk of the doomed craft by the avenging sky dragon, the falling bodies of the two they sought. Supporting the half-conscious prince above the blue waters, Charn Thovis watched the distant airboats dwindle in the distance towards Patanga many leagues away, and his heart sank within his breast. They were miles from either shore of the Gulf, and they could never manage to swim to land. Unless a miracle occurred, they were doomed . . . strange irony of Fate, to preserve them from the terrible fall from the wrecked floater, only to let them drown in the Gulf.

But a miracle had occurred, and her name was the *Scimitar,* as he soon learned. And the brawny, bronze-tanned pirate who gave him the broth was the same Thangmar who had dived from the *Scimitar's* rail to save them when the two floating bodies had been spied by a lookout aloft in the rigging.

Thangmar was a towering giant from the forest country west of Tsargol, a wooded wilderness where savage clans of the untamed Kodanga roamed and fought. He stood seven feet tall, a mighty-thewed colossus of dark bronze, his bright golden mane braided in a thick rope down his back. He grinned broadly when he saw that Charn Thovis was strong enough to stand and his strange blue eyes twinkled with friendly good-humor—strange, that is, because Charn Thovis had never seen a person with blue eyes in all his life before this. Most of the peoples of the West were of the brown-skinned, black-haired and dark-eyed Turanian race. Blond-haired, blue-eyed men were rarely met in the Nine Cities.

But then he had never encountered a Kodangan before. The Kodangans were wild barbarian warriors who shunned cities and dwelt in the unexplored Red Forest kingdom that lay on the southern coasts of Lemuria between the cities of Tsargol the Scarlet and Tarakus. Forest savages, they had a wild, fierce contempt for the ways of city-dwelling folk and much preferred their rude wooden towns with palisade walls hidden amid the trees. But Thangmar, as Charn

77

Thovis later learned, was one Kodangan who had adopted city ways. Captured as a boy by a slaving expedition from Tarakus, he had survived to become one of them and sail the high seas, preferring the wild life of a Sea Rover to the tribal existence of his own primitive people.

"You and boy well now," the blond giant said with a grin. "What you do in gulf so far from land?"

Charn Thovis thought swiftly. These corsairs were the enemies of every kingdom and had no friends among the walled cities of the gulf or the southern coast, whose shipping they attacked and plundered. Were he to reveal the true identities of Prince Thar and himself, the pirate captain of the *Scimitar* would beyond question hold Thar for ransom and sell him back to Dalendus Vool for a handsome price—they would end up back in the hands of their enemies once again, and all their struggles to escape and to elude pursuit and capture would have gone for nothing.

He looked down at himself. His cloak and boots he had discarded when he struck the water, for greater ease in keeping afloat. He had removed and flung away both the urlium harness and the electripotent sithurl crystal, fearing that immersion in the water might cause the power jewel to short-circuit. Hence, in his leathern kilt and water-soaked leathern girdle, he looked like an ordinary person and retained upon his garments no token or insignia which marked him as a fighting man of the elite Black Dragons of Patanga. As for Thar, he wore only a loin-cloth, and in his present soaked and bedraggled state looked nothing at all like a prince.

So he hastened to put together some sort of tale that would satisfy the curious crewmen without revealing there was anything special about the boy or himself.

As it happened, though, there was no need for invention on his part. The pirates were perfectly capable of creating a story of their own.

"Fisherfolk, *I* say," whined a lean and bewhiskered old seaman whose lined, dour and leathery face was seamed with the white marks of ancient cutlass scars. A crimson kerchief was knotted around his brows and a black patch hung over one empty eye-socket.

"Fell in with a sea-dragon and lost they boat," the old sailor commented further, eyeing them shrewdly with his one keen eye.

"Aye, old Durgan's hit on it," nodded a fat Kovian with a vast leathern girdle bristling with dirks and dags around his mighty paunch. His red, perspiring moon-face nodded in a kindly manner at the silent Thar, which set an immense gold hoop in his earlobe to wobbling and twinkling. "Zangabal-born, by the looks of the lad," the fat pirate puffed, pursing his lips thoughtfully. "Right, young fellow? Tell Blay the truth now!"

Before Charn Thovis could marshal his wits sufficiently to reply, a thunderous bellow from the foredeck split the air.

"*Blay,* you blubber-guts! I'll do the questioning on my own deck—Durgan, bring those two forward if they can walk, and let's see what kind of fish we've hauled up from the waves this time—hurry on, you spindleshanks!"

"Aye, Captain! Fisherfolk from Zangabal, they be," old Durgan whined as the pirates helped Charn Thovis and the boy forward. "Tossed overboard in a squall, *I* say," he added with a knowing wink.

"Well, let's have a look at them," the captain roared.

Blay, Durgan and grinning Thangmar helped Charn Thovis and Thar up the steep wooden stair to the foredeck, then fell back respectfully as their master strode forward.

"Hmm. A bedraggled pair, fry my guts if they're not," the captain grunted as he raked them up and down with fierce gray eyes under scowling tufted brows. He was an immense man, built like a bull, broad-chested, thick-necked, with sturdy massive legs and heavy arms like mighty tree-roots. The most astonishing thing about him was the vast beard that covered half his face and streamed down almost to his gem-studded girdle. It was curly as a fleece and red as raw gold. The contrast between the burning bush of beard and the leathery bronze of his deeply tanned face was startling. A gaudy kerchief of crimson and gold silk was wound about his brows. He wore breeches of bottle-green and enormous boots of black leather. A great

79

scimitar hung at his side from a baldric slung across his bare chest, which was shaggy with curly golden hair. He resembled nothing more than a towering blond bear as he stood there in the bright dawn glaring down at them.

"Who fetched 'em from the gulf—you, Thangmar?" he demanded in that great bull-throated voice that seemed to come from deep down in the monstrous girth of his belly, gathering volume as it travelled.

The Kodanga giant nodded cheerfully.

"Well, the next time you jump in the sea to save scrawny wretches such as these, the *Scimitar* sails on without you. Look at the two of 'em—not enough meat on their bones to feed the fish! Why, they'll cost us more to feed 'em up to man-size than they be worth," he grumbled. Then he fixed Charn Thovis with his frosty gray eyes, cold as fractured steel.

"If you be thinking I'll about helm and take you back to Zangabal, my lad, think again. My name be Barim of Belnarth, called Barim Redbeard by some. And just ere dawn we took a merchant galley out of Zangabal, looted her to the bare boards, and scuttled her as well. They in Zangabal would not take kindly to Barim Redbeard if he were fool enough to carry you two back—aye, they'd string us up in a moment. What d'you say to that?"

Charn Thovis forced a smile.

"Captain Redbeard, my name is Charn and this is Tharn, my brother," he said, giving the first names that came into his head. "At the moment, we are both too grateful for kindness in saving us from drowning to feel anything but thankful. May I ask, sir, what you intend doing with us?"

The burly captain subsided a little at these graceful words, and sounded a little more affable and a little less fierce as he replied: "Well, now, as for that, we're bound back to home port, and making no stops, so you'll come along with us whether you like or no! But I guess we can spare a couple of bunks and a few square meals—the little lad could use some beef on his bones, fry my guts if he couldn't!"

Thar did not like being patronized. One brown fist

clutched at his waist where his small sword would have been if it hadn't been lost during the hours they floundered through the waves.

"I'll have you know—" the boy began sharply, subsiding when Charn Thovis clutched his bare shoulder in a tight grip. The warrior forced a cough.

"My brother Tharn is still a little light-headed, Captain Redbeard. We floated for two or three hours before your ship saw us and your man Thangmar saved us from the waves . . ."

"That's all right, I like a lad with spirit," Barim Redbeard chuckled. "Well, being fisherfolk, you know your way about a deck, I fancy, and can earn your keep mopping the decks and repairing cordage, tackle and gear. Get them below, Durgan, and let the lads rest a bit and take some grub aboard those empty bellies. And now let's up sail and head for home and no more delays, or we'll have half the navy of Zangabal on our necks!"

The mate, a thickset, black-whiskered and villainous-looking little man, bellowed commands. Seamen clambered into the rigging. Sails unfurled and shook out with hollow booms, swelling as the morning breeze caught them. The *Scimitar* bent seawards under a quickening breeze.

As Charn Thovis climbed down into the cabins, he cast a last despairing glance at open sea and morning sky. He had never heard the phrase "out of the frying pan, into the fire," but he knew the reality of the dilemma. With daring, courage and ingenuity, he had managed to save Thar from the clutches of Dalendus Vool—only to fall into the hands of the dread pirates of Tarakus.

Chapter 12: A KNIFE IN THE BACK

> The night is clear, the tide is fast,
> Break out the sails once more!
> We're forth upon the sea at last
> To seek a golden shore. . . .

> —*Sea Chantey of the Pirates of Tarakus*

The pirates of Tarakus were the scourge of Yashengzeb Chun the Southern Sea and the terror of the coast. But rarely did they venture this far into the broad waters of the Gulf of Patanga. It was lucky for Charn Thovis and Prince Thar that Barim Redbeard had so dared on this occasion—else they would have drowned in the briny waves. On the other hand, they now found themselves captives, helplessly outnumbered by a crew of ferocious cutthroats who respected neither king nor law nor the very gods of heaven.

In the days that followed their rescue, Charn Thovis—or Charn of Zangabal, as he was now known—adjusted to the life of a seaman and learned much from the rough pirates. They were an uncouth lot, dirty and unkempt, their bearded lips spewing forth a constant stream of oaths and foul language. But the iron hand of Barim Redbeard held them in line, worked them hard, dealt fairly with their transgressions, broke up their frequent quarrels, and kept them away from the strong drink they craved. The corsair chieftain from Belnarth could out-fight and out-fence any man of his crew, even Thangmar, the blond giant from Kodanga, and not excepting the nine-foot-tall Blue Nomad, Roegir. Thus they feared and respected him, and

Charn Thovis came to realize that, pirate or no, Barim Redbeard was a man.

It was not easy for the young noble and his princely charge to adjust to this strange new life. As soon as they were alone on that first morning aboard the *Scimitar*, Charn Thovis had cautioned Thar to guard his tongue with care. He must forget that he had ever been the prince of Patanga. Never by act or stance or slip of tongue must he betray the fact that he was aught else than Tharn, a simple fisherman's boy from the wharves and quays of Zangabal.

The pirates were not unfriendly to the newcomers. But they worked the warrior and his prince unmercifully and made jest of the fumbling ineptitude of Charn Thovis, a novice to the seaman's craft. One of them in particular joyed in making mock of the Pantagan's mistakes. This fellow was named Gothar, a scowling, surly and black-a-vised scoundrel out of Thurdis who was always getting into brawls because of a vicious and uncontrollable temper. His right hand had been hewn off in some sea-battle. In its place he wore a leather cup over the stump and carried at his girdle a variety of tools he could screw into the grooved socket of this cup. Sometimes he used a steel hook or a sawblade. Lean and leathery old Durgan and fat, friendly Blay cautioned Charn Thovis to be wary of Gothar's vile temper. For he was a killer and had slain nine men in brawls—all of them slashed to death with the razor-keen hook he bore with him at his waist.

"Ever you see that Gothar screwin' a hook into his leather—watch yourself," Durgan warned. "That be a sign he means to kill."

Charn Thovis promised to beware of the scowling Thurdan and ordered Thar to keep clear of him. But it was not so easy as it might sound, especially as Gothar continued to make Charn Thovis the butt of his contemptuous, mocking humor. The young warrior endured as much of the foulmouthed pirate's ill usage as he could. But then came the time he caught Gothar mistreating the boy—and he could endure no more.

Young Thar had been repairing some cordage, a delicate task requiring patience and nimble-fingers. The boy's attention had strayed and he botched the job, which roused the devil in Gothar. He kicked the boy sprawling and loomed over him, spewing abuse and lifting his one hand to strike him in the face.

Charn Thovis was across the deck in two strides. He caught Gothar's shoulder in a vise-like grip, spun the surprised corsair around—and struck him twice. One balled fist caught him in the belly, just below the ribs. Breath whistled from Gothar's sallow lips and he sagged. The second blow, which rose from the level of Charn's knees, caught him square on the point of the jaw. It snapped his head back, lifted him a half-inch off his feet, and slammed him back against the rail.

Silence fell over the deck. Fat Blay rolled the whites of his eyes and Durgan choked off a curse. Charn Thovis stood waiting with fists ready. Purple with fury, Gothar climbed unsteadily to his feet, wiping a trickle of blood from his thin lips. His eyes burned into Charn Thovis with unwavering, venomous hate. One bony hand snaked to his girdle and unsnapped a cleaver-blade. The warrior felt coldness go down his spine but he stood ready to defend himself with bare hands.

Then a black shadow fell across Gothar's snarling visage and whip-leather sang as it cracked across his face. He staggered back, blood welling from a grisly welt, to meet the cold, ominous eyes of Barim Redbeard himself. The captain's eyes were frigid and gray—like a swordblade sunk fathoms deep in arctic ice. He let the whip slither restlessly across the deck.

"I've had my eye on you, Gothar," the Redbeard growled. "Now hark to me, you cowardly black dog: if ever I see or hear of you laying your dirty paws on the little lad here, I'll take this whip to your back till the ribs show white bone. Hear me? Then back to your kennel, you sneaking filth—go!"

With that, the captain turned to help Thar to his feet, contemptuously turning his back on Gothar whose vicious face had turned dirty gray at the insult. Men turned their eyes away from that face, and only Charn Thovis saw what happened next.

84

Like a great white spider, Gothar's one good hand crawled down to his waist and came up with the hook in its grip. Almost before Charn could move or speak, Gothar had set the hook in his leather-capped stump. He took one long step forward and raised his arm to drive the keen hook into the broad back of Barim Redbeard.

Charn Thovis hurled himself at that arm. Time seemed to slow to an imperceptible pace. He flung himself before the descending hook. With both hands he tried to seize the arm and turn it aside. Instead, it slid along his chest, the glittering hook slicing a red furrow through his bronzed flesh. Charn Thovis gasped at the bite of the cold steel. Muscles bunched along his shoulders. He gripped Gothar's arm and shoved it down—and back. The hook sank to its hilt in Gothar's guts. White-faced, his mouth open and working, sallow lips frothed with crimson foam, the pirate sagged to the deck. And died there with a half-finished curse on his lips.

Blood gushed from Charn Thovis' chest wound. He swayed a little on numb limbs and felt the deck wheel around him. The next thing he knew, Barim Redbeard's brawny arm was about his shoulders, easing him to a comfortable place on a heap of canvas and the captain's bull-throated voice was commanding hot water and clean cloths. With hands as gentle as a woman's, the captain bathed and cleansed the cut, and bandaged it.

He said little but his eyes spoke much. Charn Thovis realized that he had made a friend of Barim Redbeard. A friend for life.

The cut was shallow and would heal cleanly and quickly. Charn Thovis spent the day in his bunk resting, but was soon up and around. Almost at once he noticed a remarkable change in the attitude of the pirates towards himself and Prince Thar. They were aloof no longer. He had won their friendship.

For all their bloody-handed trade, they proved a kindly lot. Lonely men living a rough life with death and danger at every hand, they were fiercely loyal to their captain and eager to show their regard for the stranger who had saved

85

him from a traitor's knife in the back.

While Charn Thovis rested and felt his wound heal swiftly in the open air and salt tang of the sea-wind and the burning sun, old Durgan and fat Blay and the other pirates adopted Thar and vied with each other to teach the eager boy to clamber about in the rigging and balance on the spars.

Thangmar had been their friend from the moment he dove in the blue waters of the Gulf and bore Charn Thovis' head up out of the waves. Now the grinning, good-natured blond giant from the Red Forests of Kodanga taught Thar how to steer the great ship and handle the broad rudder that thrust into their foaming wake behind the curve of the galley's keel.

One by one the other men became friendly. Roegir, the Blue Nomad, was generally a silent, grim-faced loner who shunned the companionship of the others and seemed apart from them—perhaps due to his race, for he was the only Hordesman from the farthest East among the pirates of the *Scimitar*. But Thar had learned a few words of the Nomad dialect from Shangoth and Chundja and the other Jegga warriors who had served in Thongor's private guard. And soon the laughing boy won even the unspeaking Roegir for a friend and Charn Thovis watched as the indigo-skinned nine-foot colossus rode the boy around on his shoulders.

Even the glum, bad-tempered mate, a thickset, black-whiskered little man named Angar Zend, was won over by Charn Thovis' act and Thar's boyish merriment. He bent a benign eye on the little prince and permitted the men to teach him how to handle himself aloft. Soon the bright-eyed boy was clambering up rope ladders and treading the perilous, narrow ways aloft among the rigging as fearless and sure-footed as a monkey.

Thar was very young and youth is adaptable. The boy made friends among the pirates, to whom he became a sort of pet. They competed with one another to teach him how to splice a rope or mend a sail, taught him to handle a seaman's cutlass and to read the winds and the currents and to calculate the direction of the ship's course from the stars. Thar, who had never been on a sea-going ship in his ife, loved every minute of it. And even Charn Thovis began to relax and enjoy himself; surely he could have found no better hiding-place from the scrutiny of Dalendus Vool than here among the pirates of the Southern Sea.

From the grinning blond giant, Thangmar, he soon learned that the fierce-eyed pirate chief, Barim Redbeard, was a kindly man at heart, his raging temper and blazing glare being most bluff and brag. He found out that Barim was a Northlander from the bleak steppes of that cold country beyond the Mountains of Mommur from whence Thongor of Valkarth had come years before. He wondered what would happen if he were to reveal the truth about Thar. Perhaps the pirate was not to be trusted with so important a secret, and the greed and lawlessness of his scarlet trade would tempt him to sell the prince to his enemy. Or perhaps the tribal kinship of the Northlander and the blood-debt between them would make him a staunch and powerful friend.

Charn Thovis did not know which would prove the case. His inclination was to confide in the rough-talking but friendly buccaneer, and ask his aid, yet the secret was too valuable to risk lightly. For a time, the son of Thongor was entrusted to his keeping. In this lad lay the future of Patanga. Charn Thovis would not betray that trust. Without a moment's hesitation he would give his life to shield the boy from harm. Already, he had given much for his prince—he was an outlaw, his name and honor smirched and befouled, a traitor in the eyes of those Patanganya who did not know the truth about Dalendus Vool. He would wait and bide his time and see what was to happen.

But he must make up his mind soon. Terribly soon. For Barim Redbeard had told him what would happen to the boy and himself when they docked in the pirate port of Tarakus.

The pirate growled and tugged fiercely at his fiery mustachios, when, near the end of their voyage, Charn Thovis summoned up enough courage to ask what he would do with them when they came to Tarakus.

"Well, as for that, lad, the Law of the Red Brotherhood

of the Sea Rovers leaves me no choice," the captain grunted, avoiding Charn Thovis' eye. "Kashtar, our chieftain, demands that every captive seized or rescued, be offered at the block for open bidding."

Charn Thovis stood silent, stunned at this knowledge; although he had dreaded their arrival and half-guessed their fate, the reality was more awful than he had dared to estimate. *The Son of Thongor will become a slave,* he thought with cold despair, *and all because of my fumbling.*

"I'm sorry, lad," Barim Redbeard said gruffly. "Were it up to me, I'd have you, aye, and the little lad as well, for my crew. But what can I do—even in Tarakus, the Law rules!"

"This much I can do, and will," the Redbeard said as Charn Thovis stood silently. "For there be a debt of blood betwixt we two, and I were no man did I not discharge it honorably. 'Tis in my mind, when you and the lad your brother stand on the block, to bid and buy the two of you. Then you can join the crew and we will be shipmates together! 'Tis no more than I owe you, Charn, for that deed you did, shielding my back with your body."

Charn nodded, not trusting himself to speak. He was not ungrateful. He realized the extraordinary generosity in the Redbeard's gesture. But could he stand idly by and watch Thongor's son, the heir of Patanga, sold as a slave on the block—even though he be sold to a good friend?

What could he do to prevent it?

Barim Redbeard misunderstood his silence and clapped him a friendly blow on the shoulder, then turned to stride across the deck to bellow at a seaman aloft in the shrouds who was fouling a line.

Charn Thovis wandered down amidships and found young Thar, his black mane bound up in a seaman's red stocking-cap, a bright sash wound around his lean waist, sitting cross-legged atop a barrel watching the men dance a rude sailor's step, lifting his clear young voice to join in the roaring chorus of a bold chantey as the corsairs cavorted upon the deck.

He leaned against the rail and stared out over the tossing waves. White gulls circled in their wake, cawing raucously

League after league of empty blue water caught the fierce sunlight and hurled it back at the morning sky in ten thousand dancing shards of light.

At sunset they would dock on the long quays of Tarakus

. . .

The young chanthar cudgeled his wits to find some way of escaping from this dilemma. Search as he might, however, he could think of no answer to the problem that faced him. Every hour took Thar and himself farther and farther from the friendly cities of the upper Gulf . . . every hour took them closer and closer to the slave-pens of Taragus the Pirate City.

There was naught that he could do to prevent it. He must bend with the tide of the times, and keep a vigilant eye open for an opportunity to help the boy escape.

Dragon-prow lifting as it sliced through the brine, the *Scimitar* spread her sails full and caught the breeze, heading southward for Tarakus.

The Fourth Book

THONGOR AMONG THE GODS

"Thus did the Unknown One create the Nineteen Gods, even Gorm the Father of Stars and great Tryphondus, Aedir the Sungod and Tiandra the Lady of Fortune, Diomala of the Harvest and Illana the Moon-Lady, Karchonda of the Battles, Dyrm the Stormgod, grim Avangra and Erygon and Iondol the Lord of Song, Aslak the Godsmith, Pnoth the Lord of the Aeons and Althazon the Divine Messenger, Nergondil and Aarzoth the Windlord, Shastadion of the Sea, Zath-Lomar and bright Balkyr. Into their hands He put the force of nature and the rule of all things . . . and Lo! the world was."

—*The Lemurian Chronicles*
Book One, Chapter ii.

Chapter 13:   LORD OF STARRY WISDOM

> Gray cloudy mists about him swirled
> Into a looming form most odd;
> There, at the edge of an unknown world,
> He stood and gazed upon a God.

> —*Thongor's Saga,* Stave XVIII

A titanic face looked down on him. Overpowering awe seized his heart as he stood there at the foot of the mountainous throne, staring up at the immensity of the shadowy shape that loomed above him.

It was not unlike the face of a man, but stamped with superhuman majesty and an unearthly spiritual beauty compounded of strength and will and tremendous wisdom beyond the horizons of mortal minds.

The misty waterfall of a kingly beard streamed down the cloudy breadth of its gigantic chest. Eyes bright and keen as great stars flashed at him from the shadows of a dim hood. One mighty hand held against the figure's breast a vast book locked with seven seals. He knew that volume for the legended Book of Millions of Years, and he knew the being who clasped it to be none other than Pnoth the Lord of Starry Wisdom, the Master of the Aeons.

The Lord of Time looked down at him, and spake in a deep voice like the rumble of distant thunders.

"What dost thou in the Land of Shadows, O Swordsman of Valkarth?"

He shook back his ebon mane against the wind, and lifted the Sword of Light in the great salute men make only to the mightiest of kings.

"I am a dead man, dread Lord of the Ages, and my

shade is sent to wander here for some unknown purpose, bound from immensity unto immensity upon a quest whereof I know little."

"Dead, sayest thou?" the God of Time asked. "Hast thou learned naught from the things thou hast met in thy wanderings through this realm?"

Thongor was baffled and knew not how to answer.

"Aye, Lord, I have learned that all is not as it seems, and that the form is not the fact, in this strange Kingdom of the Shadows," he said at last. The titanic form nodded slowly, tipping its ponderous head to stare down at him with thoughtful, brooding eyes.

"Then beware how thou answerest, if the fact be not as the form sheweth," the titan form said. "For, indeed, how dost thou know that thou art here in truth, and that all about thee is not but the baseless vision of some dream? And as for death, what knowest thou of life that thou canst speak so certainly of death?

Again, Thongor knew not how to answer and stood thinking, striving to pit his mortal wits against the ageless wisdom of the phantom divinity that loomed above him seated upon the mountains as a man might sit upon a great chair. At length the Lord Pnoth spoke again in slow, thoughtful, measured tones.

"There be ten thousand states of being, O Warrior of the West, and between one state and its neighbor lieth but the thickness of a hair. Thou and thy kind in thy ignorance and folly, gather all the shades of these spectra of existence under two terms. The one thou callest 'Life,' and deem thou knowest whereof thou dost speak. The other thou callest 'Death,' and know not whereof thou dost speak. For thou in thy folly dost consider all that liveth not in the flesh as being of Death, and all that liveth in the flesh as being of Life. But the state of Being is far more than these simplicities, O Mortal, far more than thou canst dream. It were as if thou were to take the thousand hues of light and class all those that be bright as White and all the darker hues as Black. Thou utterest folly when thou dost pronounce thy thoughts on subjects whereof thou knew knowest not."

The Valkarthan frowned. A man of violent action, never

given to philosophical abstractions, he yet thought he could see some faint beam of light through the darkness that clothed the strange words of the Lord Pnoth.

"You mean then, Mighty Lord of the Aeons, that I should not take it for granted that because I seem to be in this realm of the dead—I *am* dead?" he demanded.

The cloudy visage smiled and nodded approvingly.

"If that be so, why, then, am I here and how came I to this Land of Shadows?" he asked.

"Ask not of me how that thou camest here, but take thy questions to the King of the Gods, even Gorm the Eternal, for he alone knoweth, being all-wise."

This roused in Thongor yet another question, one that had first occurred to him hours or aeons before, when he was first come before the Shadow-Gates and spoke to the mysterious being known only as the Dweller on the Threshold. There, briefly, it had occurred to him to wonder if all the tales of *The Scarlet Edda* were true. For, by all that he had ever been told of the Nineteen Gods Who Watch the World, the spirits of the valiant heroes were, on the point of death, borne aloft by the winged War-Maids through the skies unto the shining Hall of Heroes whereover ruled Father Gorm himself, the Moulder of the Earth and Maker of the Stars.

But such had not happened to him. Was there a secret buried here—a hidden meaning he was meant to puzzle out for himself? Would it serve any purpose to ask the Lord Pnoth of this, or must he think the problem through to its conclusion on his own?

Pnoth leaned forward.

"I know thy thoughts, O Man of Valkarth, and the questions that rise within thy breast. Come, let me bear thee unto the arm of my throne and show thee the way that thou must travel . . ."

One shadowy hand reached down from the mountainous heights to close about his naked form. The next moment Thongor felt himself borne aloft. Winds shrieked around him, tossing and tangling his coarse unshorn mane until it streamed behind him like a black and torn banner. The land fell away from beneath him and he felt vertigo. Sheer

93

cliffs of rugged stone flashed by him as the cloudy hand bore him in swift ascent. His senses blurred and vision faded.

He came to himself moments later. He was standing atop the crest of a mountain, one of the several that made up the titanic throne of Pnoth. The peak whereon he stood was high above the flat and desolate expanse of the Land of Shadows. From this height, the half-world he had ventured through seemed very small. Almost could he trace his path across the colorless desert from the Shadow-Gates unto the mountain throne. He could dimly make out in the misty purple gloom that shrouded Death's amazing kingdom, the length of the strange road whereon he had journeyed, and the symbolic ruins that adorned its margins. He looked around and saw with a grunt of surprise that the shadowy colossus was gone!

Strange and strange, he thought moodily. *Everything in this cursed land is a mystery . . .*

Above, the dark heavens were filled with dim twinkling stars. They were not the stars of his earthly skies, he well knew, for when he was a boy his barbarian father had taught him to read his directions from the constellations. These stars swirled into fantastic configurations utterly unknown to him—patterns devoid of name or meaning.

But far and farther still, high above the Shadowlands, he saw what must be the Hall of Heroes. Like a shining island of light it hung above the Universe, a glittering mass of blazing gold higher even than the faint, few stars that strove to light these strange heavens beyond the world he knew.

There, said legend, go the souls of heroic warriors to war and adventure forever beyond this realm of shades where the spirits of ordinary men and women find their final home. There, on that golden island in the sky, he belonged. Why, then, was he here? Could the gods err? Or was there some purpose to his quest?

He stood, head bowed, thinking. Many questions rose before him like faceless gibbering phantoms, but none of them seemed to be the questions he sought.

He looked down at the gold hilt of the Sword of Light.

94

And suddenly he glimpsed a trace of the hidden reality which all this symbolic, shadowy realm masked. Suddenly there came to him a question that struck to the very heart of the enigma.

The question was this: *why had he taken the sword?*

Indeed, why had the gods wished him to take it? For he knew now that naught occurred within this mystic realm that was without purpose or meaning, if only you knew the right questions to ask.

He cast his memory back over the events that had taken place since he passed through the Shadow-Gates. He had seen the sword and taken it. Obviously, it was set there for that purpose, to catch his eye. But since taking it—he had never once needed it!

Except (he recalled) when the ogre rose up before him . . . no, not even then! For, as he had discovered, the ogre was without real existence. It was a shadow of his own fear, and when he had throttled down that fear and conquered it, he whelmed and slew the ogre as well.

But he had slain the ogre with the sword! The sword had blazed forth into being as a shaft of dazzling light, which dispelled and drove away the black phantom of his fear. Or had this actually happened in very truth? Perhaps . . . perhaps it had been the very *act* of courage that destroyed the shadowy Ogre. Perhaps the sword itself was but the outward emblem and symbol of his courage!

A clue to this lay in the nature of the Sword of Light itself. It was not truly a sword at all, only the hilt of one. The sword became complete only when his courage rose within him, together with the determination to battle on against whatever odds seemed to face him.

He wondered if he had come at last to the truth, or to a portion of the truth, that he was expected to puzzle through. The dangers of this realm seemed only illusions: the wall of ice and the river of fire had been tricks of the senses alone, and he had surmounted those obstacles the moment he had dared to attempt them.

That seemed to ring true. But what was he supposed to realize from this? Again, his brow knotted in deep thought and he pondered in silence there on that lofty mountain-peak under the dim and distant stars.

His gold eyes flashed. *Could* it be that he was supposed to learn from these mystic experiences that life's hazards and obstacles could be as easily conquered in the world he had left behind? A trace of logic seemed discernible. Since everything in the Land of Shadows was but the analogue of an earthly counterpart, perhaps the truths of this realm shadowed forth something of the truths of life itself. . . .

Almost he was tempted to laugh at the thought. A monster dragon of primal Lemuria's steaming swamps and fetid jungles was no shadow! It was real and solid, and no matter how much courage a warrior summoned as he faced the brute, it could *still* crush him down and tread his flesh to scarlet ruin.

What, then, did this lesson mean? The kernel of truth stubbornly continued to elude his searching mind. He shrugged, and stood up. He had reached a decision. Perhaps he was acting like a fool, but . . .

He stepped to the edge of the chasm and hurled the Sword of Light away!

It fell twinkling through the dim gulf and vanished in the gloom. His only weapon was gone.

He stood, great arms folded on his mighty chest, waiting for he knew not what. He had realized the truth behind the symbol, the truth he was meant to learn. Thus, he had abandoned the symbol, knowing that he required it no longer. If any enemy challenged him, the determination to give battle and the courage to face the threat alone would suffice.

In recognition of this, he had abandoned his only defense. In essence, he had hurled a challenge in the very faces of the gods! Now he awaited some sign or omen that he had acted in the manner that the gods required of him.

He did not have long to wait—although the omen was considerably different from anything he had expected.

A shadow fell over him as he stood there on the mountain crest. He looked up, startled, to see a fantastic winged shape hurtling down out of the misty sky.

It plunged for him.

Chapter 14:   BEHIND THE STARS

> And Thongor lifted up his hand
> And hurled the shining Sword away,
> Determined here to take a stand
> And face the omen, come what may.

—Thongor's Saga, Stave XVIII

He drew back like a wild beast at bay, a deep growl rumbling in his chest. The hurtling figure suddenly spread bright wings and fluttered to the crest of the mountain throne.

Whatever it was, it was no beast. It was immensely tall—two or three times the size of a man—and radiant with dazzling light that beat about it so brilliantly that the Valkarthan must blink his eyes against the glare, and it was some moments before his bedazzled vision could make out the shape that stood there on the wind-swept mountain peak, clad with intolerable light, towering above him against the few faint stars.

The brilliance ebbed; the figure solidified from gold light. With a thrill of awe he looked upon a mighty form of superhuman beauty—a proud, eternally youthful face, hawklike in its beauty, wild and fierce and free, crowned with a silken mane whose flowing locks floated like vapors on the wind. The figure, manly, heroic, superbly proportioned, was nude but clad in veils and webs of brilliance. From shoulders, back, hips and brow nine great wings grew, and the eyes that blazed down upon him were fiercer than twin suns.

He knew it for none other than Althazon, the Herald of the Gods, for he had seen the marble likeness of that

97

superb and nine-winged form in the temples and had read of the Divine Messenger in *The Scarlet Edda,* wherein were compiled the sacred and prophetic scriptures of Lemuria.

The radiant being smiled and hailed him in a voice like great winds. "Belarba, O Warrior of the West! The Father of the Gods hath dispatched me unto the Shadowlands to bring thy spirit-self for judgment before the Throne of Thrones."

Thongor gravely acknowledged the greetings of the messenger, knowing that his decision to throw away the Sword of Light had been the proper course of action. "I am ready," he said.

"Then come, O Hero of Patanga, for the King of the Stars awaits thee in his mighty Hall."

The flight was a titanic quest through the star-thronged Universe. The bright-winged figure bore him up from the crest of the mountains and they flew aloft on thundering pinions while the Land of Death fell away beneath them. Great winds roared about them as they clove the air asunder. Darkness came, that vast and limitless Night that lies in ebon gulfs between the shining suns . . . blackness such as mortal man hath never known, nor shall, till that far distant day when his great fleets sweep up from the bosom of this world and dare the darkness and the deeps beyond the stars.

Thongor felt the winds die, but a sensation of unthinkable speed assaulted his senses. He was aware of a velocity beyond measure or knowledge. In the blinking of an eye that whole vast realm wherethrough he had wandered and adventured dwindled to a fleck of dust and was lost in the bleak immensities of the stellar void.

Vast wings beat about him and his black mane flowed behind, but he knew that still was his mind bemazed with analogue and symbol. Bereft of the body, his spirit-self quested in regions beyond the reach of the senses, yet his merely human mind was not capable of seeing and grasping the realities of this region, and hence interpreted the meaningless nerve-signals in familiar terms. He knew the bright being who bore him through the star-spaces was not really bewinged as some lowly fowl of earth and air, nor did those shining pinions flap in truth, beating against the winds that blow between the worlds. But how else to grasp the sense of flight, save in recognizable symbols?

Now was the universe spread out about him, like the ransom of a thousand emperors in burning jewels, heaped and strewn on black velvet. More stars than ever he knew adorned the breast of heaven dazzled him with their supernal splendor.

Many were blue-white, like scintillant diamonds, but others shone topaz-yellow like the eyes of lions, grass-green like glowing emeralds, or scarlet as bright rubies. Colors beyond name or number blazed about him in gemmed magnificence . . .

Now, as they ascended with unthinkable speed to a higher coign of vantage, he could see the stars were caught up in vast curving arms that formed a spiral of dazzling glory. Thongor's primitive people were ages from a science of astronomy, and knew naught of galaxies, but now he looked upon that tremendous wheel of light we call the Milky Way.

Suns flashed past them, swelling to rondure as they ascended, roaring by like blazing furnaces, and dwindling behind them. Marvelous comets hurtled past in arches of pale light, as if the hand of some supernal artist, dipping his brush in liquid light, had drawn a radiant curve across the dark canvas.

Planets sped past beneath them, and some were dead husks of frozen stone while some weird ocean worlds of limitless seas wherein enormous dragons fought and fed. Others were forest-worlds where towering armies of great trees marched rank by rank from pole to pole. And some were desert where naught moved but the whispering wind rustling over scarlet and ochre dunes of eternal and endless sand. But some, he caught a fleeting glimpse, were green and fertile worlds and very like unto his own far, half-forgotten world, where manlike beings, or beings risen from other creatures than the simian, ruled in splendid cities or fought in cataclysmic wars that laid whole continents in ruin.

Now the galaxy shrank behind them to a tiny fleck of light, and its near neighbors thundered by . . . galaxies by the score and the hundreds, rivers of suns, oceans of worlds, galaxies in their thousands and their millions streamed past as countless as the bubbles that rush over the brink of some cosmic Niagara.

Yet still onward they flew, and on, through the jeweled immensities of night. . . .

After a time, Thongor became aware they had crossed some subtle barrier. The darkness through which they now ascended was veined with faint light that was not of the billion, billion suns, for those lay beneath them like a colossal sea of stars that stretched from the brink of infinity to the edge of eternity.

They had gone behind the stars and Thongor stared now at sights whereon no intelligence would ever gaze, in a place to which came naught that could ever return to tell the wonders they had looked upon.

The sky arched above them, filled with a haze of faint dim hues, moving mists of colored light straited and granular and very different from the light that shines on men in their worlds of matter. They had quested beyond the very universe to realms of pure thought. And before them rose a shining land, an island of glory that Thongor had glimpsed from afar with the eyes of the spirit when the Lord Pnoth had raised him to the heights of the mountain that he might look upon the Hall of Heroes where the shades of the valiant dwell forever.

It opened before them. Golden summery fields and velvet meadows where bright rivers ran and strange beasts roamed and birds and fabulous monsters known to no earthly mythology flew and fought and dwelt.

These were the Shining Fields, he knew, where heroes wandered and warred forever in the eternal springtime of an endless youth whose clean strength could never dim to faltering age, but stood forever bright and unbroken.

Here they roamed on quests beyond imagination, for goals untold in legend, or battled in magnificent wars, or feasted in a realm where satiety was unknown.

Somewhere among those glittering ranks below, he knew his grandsire, Valgoth, his mighty father, Thumithar, and the bold, strong brothers of his youth, dwelt forever beyond death—they and other stalwart champions as well, Valkh the Black Hawk, the father of Thongor's people, and the heroes of Nemedis and the First Kingdoms of Man, and that gallant band of victors who fought and conquered the Dragon Kings of Hyperborea in The Thousand Year War, Jaidor and Khorbane and Diombar the Singer, Konnar and Yggrim, and all the great Sons of Phondath the Firstborn, whom Gorm molded from the dust of the earth in the days when the world was new.

And he would take his place among them, he knew, to dwell in the Shining Fields forever.

Amidst the bright land rose a vast structure hewn of beautiful light. They flew towards it across the Land of Heroes and as they neared, Thongor knew that he looked upon the Palace of the Gods, and a great awe gripped him and he was beyond speech.

They flew over a murmuring forest of darkly golden trees and gently as a settling leaf, Althazon the Herald of Heaven descended to stand on a hill that rose from a quiet meadow that lay sleek and glossy like rich satin, starred with small unearthly flowers.

Here the Divine Messenger bade him farewell and was gone in a thunder of glittering plumes.

Thongor stood alone and looked upon the Palace of Paradise.

The mind of mortal man could not conceive of its radiant beauty. Its unearthly splendor was such that his mind could find no analogue to represent it. So it stood, crowned with sky-tall towers, a blaze of bright beauty, beyond description. Like frozen music it was, or an epic song hewn of utter light, or a tapestry of woven thunders.

He went down the gentle slope of the hill towards it, through sweet-scented grasses where strange flowers nodded, and crossed the meadow towards the bright battlements in a golden twilight where immortal birds sang softly.

Chapter 15: THE LORD OF THE THREE TRUTHS

> The Winged One lifted him away
> Above the worlds in soaring flight—
> Beyond the ramparts of the Day,
> Beyond the battlements of Night,
>
> To where the Gods in splendor dwell
> Above the thronged and mighty suns;
> As one ensorcelled by some spell,
> He stood before the Timeless Ones.
>
> —*Thongor's Saga*, Stave XVIII

The floor beneath his feet was like a sea of glass. Black as night it stretched away from him into dim vastnesses. And, as if he hung suspended in space above the universe, gazing down he saw that within the glistening surface of the crystal pave points of light flashed like remote stars.

Here, where he had expected infinite light, was a dim mystic gloom, murmurous with echoes, mysterious with limitless vistas veiled in darkness and ever-deepening shadows. *Perhaps,* he thought, *the splendors herein are so brilliant as to be beyond brightness; here, where Glory sits, is light so intense that it seems as darkness to the astounded sense.*

The hall about him was tremendous. Mountains could have sheltered beneath that arching dome of shadows above. Pillars so thick about that one could not grasp the fact of their rondure soared unendingly into the darkness of infinite heights above.

All was silence and gloom and vast shadowy immensities. He strode forward across the glistening crystal of the night-starred floor, and, after a time whose internal he could not measure, he came into the very midst of the Hall.

Were those—thrones? In the dimness he could not make them out, but towering shapes rose in a vast circle. They seemed . . . untenanted.

One throne, if thrones they were, stood mightier than the rest. Shaped from some vast jewel, it seemed, but his eyes could see nothing in this mystery of shadows, where forms and shapes twisted away, eluding precise definition. He looked upon dimensionless and immaterial enigmas beyond human comprehension.

He became aware of a Presence.

The central throne, vaster than the others, held a Darkness. A cloud without shape or substance, a blur beyond sight. But within it an Intellect vast and calm and ageless observed him. A Brilliance, so intense that it seemed to him dark, was throned in that titanic chair.

And a Voice spake.

Strangely—in this place of strangeness—it did not thunder as had the voice of Pnoth, neither did it roar like the rushing rivers of the wind as had the voice of Althazon. It spake softly, quietly, as might one man speak to another that stood close by. Almost was it a whisper—and he had expected the thunder of ten thousand trumpets.

Perhaps, even as there is a light so brilliant that it can be perceived only as darkness, so is there a voice so mighty that it seemeth almost to be of the silence . . .

"What have you learned?" It asked.

He paused before answering, gathering his thoughts. He made no salute or obeisance before the Throne, for he could think of so gesture humble enough wherewith to acknowledge that he stood before Utter Majesty. Hence he stood straight and tall, as a man should stand, erect and proud in the Presence of Him Who Molded Man. And his answer, when it came, was spoken boldly in a clear voice.

"I have learned the lesson of the sword," Thongor said to his God. "I was puzzled that the sword should be set in my path, and knew there was a reason for this, that I was to learn something from it. First I discovered that I did not

103

truly need the sword at all—that the ability to stand before fear, to crush it down, to summon courage out of it—these were enough wherewith to conquer. I learned also not to despise fear, for courage cometh out of it."

"That was the First Truth," the Voice said quietly.

"But I questioned the meaning of what I had learned," Thongor confessed. "Since everything I met in the Land of Shadows was the echo or reflection of its counterpart in the Lands of Men, I wondered how this truth applied to the world from whence I had come. Well did I, of all men, know that in my world dangers and enemies are all too real . . . they do not vanish like empty shadows before a display of courage, as the Ogre of Fear vanished when I conquered my own fear, whose outward semblance it was."

"And what did you learn from these thoughts?"

Thongor frowned, striving to phrase his muddled thoughts clearly. "I . . . I think that I was meant to come to *this* conclusion: that the First Truth applies even to the real and physical terrors of my world as well. That it does not really matter, from the viewpoint of the gods, if one conquers and slays the dangers that one faces with courage. That true victory is not won only by him who walks away alive from a struggle. That, in the sight of the gods, the man who fights boldly and with courage and determination in a right cause is *always* the victor, whether he conquer or be conquered in the end. I learned, in other words, not to dread defeat, for victory sometimes cometh out of the midst of it!"

"That was the Second Truth, and a greater than the first," the Voice said calmly, and Thongor felt an enormous relief go through him. He had come two-thirds of the way; one last trial lay before him.

"And have you learned anything more?" the Voice asked gently. He nodded hesitantly. "The truths that I have learned during my sojourn in these strange, symbolic realms of the spirit seem to connect into a sequence of logic. Nothing here can be taken at its face value; everything I have seen or experienced is but a semblance and a symbol of an inner reality. Hence, since the Laws of

Life seem to be that differing states are but the *observe* of each other and not the *opposite* of each other—since courage grows out of fear, and victory is found even in the very midst of defeat, I am led to believe that life cometh out of death itself!"

There was a long interval of silence before the Voice again spoke.

"That was the Third Truth, and the greatest truth of all," the God said softly. "Know that you alone of all men have searched out and captured in words The Three Truths. We are very proud of you, Thongor of Valkarth."

Thongor frowned. Something was lacking—there was another link to the chain of reason he had slowly and painfully forged. What was the inescapable conclusion now forced upon him by the sequence of the Truths? Of *course*.

He turned to face the throne once again. Now he stood on the threshold of a daring revelation.

"There is one thing more, Lord," he said gropingly. "Since first I entered these curious realms, the realization of it has been growing stronger within me. Now I must know the truth of it at last—and I bring the question of it before you, the Lord of Life."

"Ask what you will," the Voice whispered.

Thongor drew a deep breath. "Since first I stepped between the Shadow-Gates, questions have risen within my heart. Always have I been taught by saga, myth and tale, that the winged War-Maids bear the souls of the valiant through the skies to the Hall of the Heroes. But such was not the case with me, who came before the gates as a wandering phantom and strove to find my own way unto this place where I might stand before thy throne."

"Yes? Speak on, and be not afraid."

"I was not struck down to death by the sword of an enemy or by the ills of the flesh nor the accumulations of age," he continued. "And I have learned in this place to take nothing at face value, not even, I suppose, the simple fact of my presence here. Hence am I forced to the conclusion that—I know not how it be, nor why, but—*I am not dead!*"

The darkness stirred. Brightness seeped from it. Reality

swayed and became transparent. The solid floor underfoot became insubstantial. He could see through the floor as through a thin veil of dimness. The walls, the prodigious columns, the gloom-thronged and vaulted dome far above, even the mighty thrones in their colossal circle became as a film of shadows.

Thongor did not know what was happening, but he felt no fear. His own spirit-self was become insubstantial too, was become as a shape of mist, a wisp of vapor, floating on the face of the deep. Far below him he could see the billion-starred expanse of the vast universe outspread. It rushed up towards him, expanding with fantastic speed. Stars hurtled by like blazing rockets—worlds and moons rushed past like the froth on the surface of a rushing river—all of the limitless universe roared about him thunderously. Yet still could he hear, above the clangorous music of the universe, the small, soft, quiet Voice as it whispered to his sense a truth more astounding than all those he had yet learned—nine words that confirmed his most incredible suspicions, and set his reason reeling with a storm of questions. Nine words that rang and echoed through his mazed, bewildered mind—

"That, too, is truth, Thongor. You are not dead."

Then, as he hurtled down, as the cosmos flashed by all about him, a fantastic panorama exploded before his astounded gaze.

He saw the mighty Universe of Stars roll up like a scroll.

The Gates of Eternity swung open to receive his flashing spirit and the silent shadow of his Companion.

He was bound on a new voyage . . . *to the End of Time.*

Chapter 16: A BILLION TOMORROWS

> Now had the mighty quest began—
> Ages unfolded to his sight—
> The epic of the Tale of Man
> Rose out of darkness into light!

> —*Thongor's Saga*, Stave XVIII

He looked down upon the world, as it was in the beginning. A vast and whirling cloud of cold matter spinning through aeons of time. Veiled in cosmic dust, he watched the whirling mass condense slowly into Being.

The great sun burned raw and young. Shouting tongues of flame leapt from its fiery surface. Not the warm golden sun he knew, but a thing of new white fire, as it had been in its youth before the worlds were made.

Six billion years before his own birth, he watched as Earth was born out of the black womb of space.

Whirling storms of dust coagulated, solidified, gathered into cold dark conglomerate. Ages passed . . . millions of tons of dust settled into matter . . . and Earth grew into a sphere of dead inert stone, bombarded by rains of meteors and storms of dust drawn by the force of gravitation.

Tons upon tons of rock crushing down caused rocks beneath to become heated, to collapse, to melt. Subterranean pockets of fiery gas and underground rivers of molten lava seethed with frustrated pressure under the crushing weight from above. After ages they burst free to the surface in thundering belts of volcanoes, in geysers that spread a boiling atmosphere of hot vapors across the earthquake-riven surface of the new planet.

Ranges of mountains lifted into being. The broken landscape was swept by fiery storms. Vapors met and mingled and cooled. Century-long rains drenched the rocky land. Seas of bubbling water condensed into being. A thousand ages passed, while the pounding waves broke and crumbled the rocks into a fine dust. The seething vapors released to the surface by volcanic action had consisted of methane, nitrogen and ammonia. Later, oxygen came into being, as the searing rays of the sun pouring down on the new atmosphere, the naked rock, the bubbling seas, added solar heat to the vast cauldron of the young world. Out of this boiling ferment of gas and liquid rock, lashed by cosmic rays, heated by the stellar furnace of the sun, new elements and new combinations of elements came into being. The poisonous vapors of the atmosphere, methane and ammonia, bathed in the sun's ultraviolet rays, slowly synthesized into amino acids, then into protein, finally in protoplasm.

Life was born.

A thousand ages swept over the primal earth. Green jungles and steaming swamps covered the face of the world. Out of the muddy seas wriggled a million living things, multiplying, fighting, dying in the slime of the Dawn Age.

Life rose, and conquered. The mighty dragon-lizards of the Morning of the World bestrode the young planet, and bellowed defiance to the stars.

The world struggled in the grip of colossal climactic forces. Ages of chilling cold swept down over the raw land, the titanic glaciers of the Ordovician and the Devonian and the Permian epochs. Bludgeoned under changing temperatures, life was forced to adapt or die. Many forms died. Some survived through change.

In the great island of Hyperborea at the North Pole an age of tropic heat flourished while the axis of the planet swung to a new configuration. There, out of the great dragons of the dawn, arose intelligence, and the dread *Narghasarkaya*—the "Dragon Kings"—came to dominate the world. With their cold, cruel, reptilian minds they probed into the darkest secrets of matter and energy, of space and time, and puzzled out the laws of black magic. Soon, leagued with dark powers of Chaos beyond the universe, they bent their cunning intelligence towards conquest and power, and a Dark Empire rose on the polar continent.

But the Gods Who Watch the World lifted their hands and the age of ice came down and whelmed all of Hyperborea beneath the eternal snows. The Dragon Kings fled south across the surging waters of an unknown sea, and came to the green shores of Lemuria which had risen from the main in a previous age. Here again the Dark Empire of the Dragon Kings spread subtle tentacles of power and sought to dominate the planet forever.

Then there came to pass that which was written aeons later in the First Book of *The Lemurian Chronicles*:

Yea, the Nineteen Gods Who Rule The World were exceeding wroth to see that the Earth was become the domain of the Dragon Kings, and they vowed that this should not be. And they spake amongst themselves in their high place above the world, speaking one to the other from tall thrones amidst the stars, saying, Let us create Man, that he may overwhelm the Children of the Serpent and break asunder the citadels of their power, and drive them utterly from the Earth, and, Lo! it was even so in the fullness of time.

Thus in time's dawn arose Phondath, Firstborn Of All Men. Out of the Earth was he sprung, yea, the flesh of his body was molded of the soil, and from the rock of the mountains were his bones made. The waters of the sea became his blood, and the breath of his body was of the airs of heaven. And Gorm the Father of Gods and Men struck within him a spark of the Fire Of Life, and Lo! he was alive upon the Earth, and his son Arniak after him, who was the father of Zuth who begat Iogrim . . .

As Thongor gazed down, he watched the First Men being armed by the gods and taught the arts of war and those of peace. The mighty tapestry of The Thousand Year War unfolded before him, that grim and glorious epic wherein the mightiest heroes of the First Kingdoms of Man went up in red war against the overwhelming power of the Dragon Kings and fought and fell, or fled to turn and fight again.

Century on century went past, and the war moved inexorably towards its victorious climax. For the world was changing, the climates swung and altered, Earth's poles froze and the axis of the planet became centered in the polar realms. And the age of the mighty reptiles was passing. In their millions the great dinosaurs were dying, and the Dragon Kings were passing, too, for all their magic and superhuman science. The great thunder dragons of the steaming Jurassic were doomed. The clock of the aeons ticked on and the world entered the Age of Mammals. Across the world animals evolved and reptiles fell. Only here in primal Lemuria the last few dinosaurs survived in the sweltering jungles and fetid swamps of the savage continent.

Eventually, Man triumphed and the Dragon Kings were conquered, and the dreaded *Narghasarkaya* of prehistoric Lemuria died out, to be remembered only in scraps as fragments of primal myth—as in the legends and epics of prehistoric India, where they are dimly remembered as the *Nagas,* the Serpent-Kings.

Thongor watched as the Children of Phondath settled the vast breadth of the Lemurian continent, the first home of mankind. He watched as the Seven Cities of the East were abandoned, and he saw the Nine Cities of the West rise in all their youth and glory.

And he saw his own coming unto the West, and the great deeds of conquest and heroism he had wrought in years gone by. Ever at his side the shadowy Companion of his quest beyond time whispered to him . . .

"Have you never wondered, Thongor, of the amazing luck that has been yours, the unconquerable fortune that followed you through all those years of wandering, adventure and war? Time and again have you miraculously escaped from amidst a thousand perils, where another man would have faltered and fallen. But the Gods have watched over you and lent you courage and wisdom and strength to aid you in the extremity of your danger. Why have we done this? For the answer to that riddle, look again on the world you know. You have seen the story of the past—now gaze upon the unborn ages of the Future."

He had built the young Empire of the West, and city after city of his foes fell before his black-and-golden banners, until at last the Nine Cities of the West were his. He watched as the reign of his stalwart young son, Thar, opened, and under the wise rule of the Son of Thongor the West basked in the glory of a Golden Age.

With an emotion almost beyond description, Thongor watched the wedding of Prince Thar, and the birth of Thandar. When the long and adventurous reign of Thar grew towards its end and the kingship of Thandar began, he watched as the unconquerable flying navy of the West explored and settled and colonized the breadth of Lemuria, desert and forest, mountain country and jungle land, wilderness and swamp. New cities grew into being, new sciences were born. Sharn, the son of Thandar, and Valkor, and Thangoth, and the kings that came thereafter spread the rule of the Golden Empire across the mighty seas . . . he looked upon unborn ages of the distant future as colonies of Lemuria the Great arose on the shores of unknown Mayapan and primal Shamballah and upon the Roof of the World in mysterious Tibet.

He saw the Last Days, when all of Lemuria foundered and sank beneath the thundering waves of the all-conquering seas. But he saw the Great Migration when the peoples of Lemuria fled by air across the world to settle in new lands, spurning beneath their keeps the foundering continent. He saw the heroic struggles of his own distant descendant, Vandar, Prince of the Last Days, to preserve the ancient wisdom.

He watched the rise of Atlantis, that island far to the east around the curve of the world. He saw the Empire of Caiphul rise to its height, and the age of Zailm Numinos. He saw the Second Empire fall before Thelatha the Demon King, as the White Emperor was driven from the City of the Golden Gates into exile. He watched as The Black Star

111

went into hiding and the long age of darkness swept over the Sacred Land.

He saw the coming of Crysarion the Restorer and those bright days wherein the White Throne was wrested from the Dark One and the Star was found, and the Empire of Adalon rose to magnificence . . . and he saw it dwindle, that Third Empire, and its glory fade as the Atlanteans fell away from their gods to grovel before the dark forces. He looked on as the reign of Phorenice the Last Empress passed slowly. He heard the Curse of Zaemon and saw the Sacred Mountain wreathed in flame. He watched as the cataclysm broke the White Isle asunder and whelmed it beneath the thundering waters of the main and the Divine Dynasty fell at last.

He saw the flight of Dakalon and Vara from the doomed land . . . those survivors who were afterwards remembered in the legends of the Greeks as Deucalion and Pyrrha, the two survivors of the Deluge. He saw them arrive at the great Atlantean colony at Sais on the delta of the Nile in the Land of Mizraim. He saw their mighty airship land, bearing the precious books and instruments, and rejoiced that something of the Sacred Records were preserved, that not all of the ancient wisdom was lost, and that only a portion of the secret science would be forgotten. . . .

He stood at last upon the end of time, the brink of the ages, where the long saga of the prehistoric world came to its end, and history begins.

He saw the walls of Babylon builded. He watched the rise of Ur of the Chaldees. He looked on as Narmer the Mighty led his legions to conquest, and the Upper and the Lower Kingdoms were united under the Double Crown, and the kingdom of Egypt was born.

Then darkness came down and obscured the Future from his sight, and he knew that the quest was ended.

The voice was speaking softly by his side as the mists of time veiled the future from his sight.

"You were singled out for the greatness that was born within you, Thongor of Valkarth. Aeons of evolution wrought within the very plasm of your seed the greatness for which the Gods strived, courage and vision, manhood and strength, wisdom and justice. From your loins shall spring a mighty line of kings, as you have seen. Your hand has set into motion the ponderous wheel of time. Under your reign, *The Golden Empire of the Sun* shall be founded, and that Empire shall outlive the very continent of Lemuria, aye, the Kings of your House shall reign in the rose-red cities of the Maya-Kings and Aegyptus on the Nile, and great Atlan. The laws you shall promulgate in your wisdom, the wars you shall fight to establish the rule of right, the sciences and arts that you shall foster, will begin a great tradition whose lore and law and learning shall go down the ages. Upon them shall be builded empires and civilizations that shall stand forever. You are the founder of human civilization, the First Hero, the King of the Dawn.

"The dim, distorted memory of your mighty deeds shall echo down the ages of the unborn Future for all time. Men shall call you Kukulkan and Odin, Herakles and Siegfried, Rama and Prometheus. The broken, half-forgotten epic of your age will live on dimly remembered in the pre-Sanskrit *Purānas,* the mythological sagas and histories of the nomadic Aryan peoples who shall spring from that wave of the Lemurian migration who shall flee the doom of their continent into the fastnesses of Asia.

"Return, then, O Thongor, to your body. For you are not truly dead. Nor can you yet die, for the empire is but half-founded and you have mighty works to complete before we can welcome your great warrior's spirit into the Hall of Heroes to dwell in the land of the immortals through measureless eternities of golden spring.

"Return, and take up your burden! For black Mardanax yet lives, and even now, a traitor forces your queen to become a bride, and the son of your loins, in whom the future of mankind resides, dwelleth in great danger. Return, O Thongor, to rise up from the tomb and do battle against your enemies . . ."

He fell through a whirling chaos of mighty mists that

swirled into a roaring vortex of confusion, split apart by thunders that seemed to rock the very stars from their places . . . down . . . down he hurtled . . . to the stone tomb that held his cold clay.

The dream (if dream it were) was ended. And life began again.

The Fifth Book

AT SWORD'S POINT

"Swiftly the flying fingers of that masked, unknown and faceless Destiny that triumphs even over the all-mighty Gods, weaveth together the threads of many different lives into a portion of that mighty Tapestry of Time; and in that vast and never-ending web wherein all men are minor figures in a grand design, it is given unto none of us to comprehend the ending of the pattern wherein the strands of our days and lives are woven. Could but we read the outcome of the tale, would not we strive to change the sequence and rewrite the ending thereof? Alas—even the Eternal Gods know not the ending of the Tale!"

—*The Scarlet Edda*

Chapter 17: IN THE PIRATE CITY

The black flag flies atop our mast,
  Our sharp prow cleaves the foam.
We're done with voyaging at last,
  We see the cliffs of home . . .

—*Sea Chantey of the Pirates of Tarakus*

The sunset spread tapestries of bloody crimson across the storm-black skies. A long and rugged promontory of bleak rock thrust from the southern coast of Lemuria into the raging waters where the great Gulf of Patanga mingled her waves with the mighty currents of Yashengzeb Chun the Southern Sea.

The uttermost tip of this rock-based promontory lifted sheer cliffs above the thunderous waves that broke in sheets of blinding foam against long quays of wet stone. The crest of the cliffs and the sides thereof were covered with a strange city whose red-tiled roofs rose level by level above the pounding waters of the main.

Tarakus the Pirate City was built like a fortress. Tall square towers lifted against the glory of the sunset sky. Frowning walls and mighty battlements ringed in the rude stone city. Nestled within the curve of the cliffs, huddled in the wall-like embrace of the great stone quays, half a score of great ships rode at anchor. Caravels and carracks, long dragon-prowed galleys and high-pooped ships of war—the most terrible sea-going fleet of all the West—the dread armada that guarded the Pirate Empire from her enemies.

The *Scimitar* came up to the mouth of the sheltered bay, where great chains sealed the entrance-way from unwarranted intruders. Barim Redbeard bellowed orders.

116

Signal lamps at prow and masthead flashed green and white and crimson in the gathering dusk, and watchful guards loosed the bronze chains that she might enter the harbor and moor along the length of the long stone quays.

Another voyage had ended, and the *Scimitar* was safe and snug in her home port—moored in the harbor of the only city of all the West where lawless outlaws ruled a kingdom of wild corsairs.

Captain, crew and captives came ashore in a longboat, and Charn Thovis and Prince Thar entered the great stone city of the pirates.

Sunset flame died; black storm-clouds thickened, piling in the west. The stars came forth, blazing in icy splendor. They strode up the great stone stairs and stood in the cobbled streets of Tarakus.

Sheltered in the curve of rocky cliffs, the pirate port blazed with light. Lanterns swung in the breeze. Greasy windows flared with light of roaring fires within. The crude stone city roared with song and thunder defiance against the cold mockery of the watchful stars—for the Sea Rovers were in port and every ale house and wineshop and inn was filled with rough swaggering corsairs roaring for food and strong drink and spoiling for a fight.

Men of half a hundred nations brawled and swaggered through the narrow cobbled alleys and twisting ways of the outlaw city. Clamped against walls of salt wet stone in iron brackets, oil-soaked torches flared, streaming long gold flames on the briny wind. Wineshop signs swung and creaked on the salty breeze before low oaken doors. They were crudely painted with emblems—crossed cutlasses, grinning skulls, the rude likenesses of sea-dragons and strange monsters.

The stormy night was filled with drunken song and revelry, loud with thunderous curses and the clash of steel on steel as drunken corsairs battled with glittering scimitars under the flaring torches, egged on by rowdy, cheering comrades. Surf boomed and roared at the foot of rocky cliffs. Salt spray exploded against wet black rocks and long stone piers and the whistling sea wind carried its icy splatter through the gusty crooked streets that wound past tall high-gabled stone houses and thick-walled adobe buildings with peaked roofs of scarlet tiles set with high narrow windows of diamond-panes.

For more than a century the little stone town sheltered in the cliff-walled cove had been the wide-open capital of a corsair empire that scourged and ruled and roved the southern seas. Here no law ruled but that bloody pact called the Articles of the Red Brotherhood. Beyond those simple codes of justice, there was no law in all of crimson Tarakus but the rule of the naked cutlasses, the clenched fist, the fighting skill of each snarling buccaneer—for the hand of every ruffian of Tarakus was lifted against the other and Might alone prevailed in the walled fortress city.

Tonight the pirate port was ablaze with mirth and song. Oaken doors hung open and the rich glare of roaring fires lit the streets and painted monstrous black shadows over the walls of the one and two-story houses. Great haunches of beef turned sizzling on creaking staves above lusty fires that crackled and seethed on stone hearths. Steel flickered and sang as duels exploded all over the streets. Rings of howling men encircled cursing duelists who fought to the death under the blazing stars over a fancied insult or an imaginary slight. Painted, giggling wineshop sluts and haggard wenches draped in the jewels of an empress clung to the bare brawny arms of bravos, cheering on the battling swordsmen.

Aye, it was a night of a thousand nights! For half the corsairs of the southern seas were in port, the ships were in and bobbing at the quays, their holds gorged with bright barbaric treasure looted from a hundred merchant ships—and the city was one brawling, lawless riot under the leering moon.

As Barim Redbeard led the way, buffeting drunken corsairs from his path, pausing to plant a smacking kiss on the crimson lips of a tavern wench, hailing and being hailed by old friends and foes, stopping to down a proffered tankard of sour ale, the party from the *Scimitar* made their slow way up the steep stairs that connected one climbing level of the city to the next. Charn Thovis was bewildered, dazed by the noise, the chaos of mirth and riot and song, the blaz-

118

ing light and gusty winds that screamed through the narrow, crowded ways. Young Thar clung to his side, eagerly drinking in the fantastic spectacle—the filthy, rough-bearded corsairs hung with incredible wealth of glittering jewels and precious metals, their bedraggled women, gowned and jeweled like savage queens, the shouts and foul curses, rude oaths and obscene ballads that filled the stormy air with noise.

Over all the thronged and crowded streets with their jostling, drunken, quarrelsome horde, over all the smoky inns and ale houses, above the narrow roofs and peaked gables, brooded the dark citadel that crowned the crest of the cliffs and thrust squat towers against the storm-dark skies where few stars flashed.

This, old Durgan told the boy and his companion, was the keep of Kashtar—cruel, sardonic, cunning Kashtar, the Red Wolf of the Sea Rovers—Kashtar the Pirate King. Of his nation and origin, there were a thousand whispered legends—but no man knew the truth thereof. He had gained power over the captains of the Brotherhood through his utter fearlessness and fighting courage, his superior command of seamanship and war tactics, his cold-blooded cruelty and sly, savage cunning. Here in Tarakus, Kashtar ruled with an iron hand, and even the wild corsairs dreaded his silken voice and subtle tongue.

Barim halted at last before a great inn whose creaking wooden sign bore the emblem of a galleon of flames. Within, a great fire roared on the grate and a bullock sizzled on the spit above a bed of glowing coals. Seamen from many cities sprawled on long low benches before grease-stained tables covered with a clutter of bottles. They roared a bawdy welcome to the mighty Redbeard, who grinned hugely and answered them in kind.

The eager crewmen of the *Scimitar* entered the inn, greeting old comrades and finding places for themselves before the blazing fire, calling for wine and roast meat and loaves of black bread. Barim cleared a place at the table for Charn Thovis and young Thar by booting four drunken sailors onto the filthy stone floor, and brushing a dozen empty bottles aside with a sweep of his brawny arm.

"Come, lads! Seat yourself—soak up some of that fire and get the chill out of your bones—eat, drink, enjoy yourselves—Barim Redbeard pays the toll, so fill your bellies!" he roared lustily. Then, reading the grim expression on Charn Thovis' face, he chuckled. "Aye, I know what chews at your guts, lad—put the slave block out of mind! That be a worry for tomorrow—tonight, well, we'll have warmth and jollity and song, a full belly and a tankard of ale and a long sleep—and dawn be hours and hours away!"

Morning came at last. Dawn filled the crooked narrow streets with thick white mist and the sky yearned blue and infinite and tender above the beetling cliffs and the brooding stone castle that clung to the rocky crest. White gulls rode the morning breeze on outstretched pinions and bright banners fluttered gaily from masthead and tower-top and wall.

With the other captives taken by the pirate fleet, Thar and Charn Thovis were stripped to their loin-cloths and led to the bazaar of slaves. They stood in the bright, baking sun, awaiting their turn on the block where a fat, black-bearded auctioneer paraded each captive in turn, loudly calling the attention of his audience, who lounged on silken cushions in the shade of orange and green awnings, to this or that good point of each slave.

Lean, one-eyed Durgan and fat, wheezing Blay and the grinning blond giant, Thangmar, came to visit and to console them as they stood in line for the slave block.

Thar, not fully understanding what was going on—slavery was unknown in Patanga, for Thongor had sweated under the overseer's lash in his time, and detested the loathsome traffic in human cattle and had forbidden it by law—peered around with keen interest at the lordly captains of the Brotherhood as they lounged in the shade.

One bower was more luxurious than the rest. In it, under hangings of imperial purple, sat a slim, foppish man with a great ruby like a hot coal smoldering in one earlobe. He was clothed in scarlet satin like a glove and his sallow smooth skin was glossy as old parchment. His face, sardonic and cold and sly, with slitted eyes of black fire, observed all and missed nothing. By his side stood a tall figure robed in neutral gray, bearing a staff of black wood carven with weird symbols, his skull-like head shaven and his face coldly impassive. His eyes, dark and keen, searched through the throng and Thar noticed how men avoided those eyes.

Blay and Durgan followed Thar's interested gaze.

"Who are those two men?" Charn Thovis asked.

"Why, the one in the red satin be our chieftain, Kashtar the Red Wolf," Blay puffed. "The bald one beside him, all in gray, be his pet wizard, Belshathla."

"Belshathla? A curious name. I cannot guess his nation," Charn Thovis mused. Fat Blay shook his head, earhoops bobbling in bright sun.

"He be from one of those Eastern countries, round abouts Darundabar or Dalakh. Nianga, now that I think on it. Beware of *that* one, lad! He be as cold and treacherous as a snake."

Almost as if some inner sense alerted him to the fact that he was the topic of their converse, the dark keen eyes of the gray wizard, Belshathla, turned upon them. The wizard's gaze passed over the three corsairs without interest, lingered a moment on the tall strong figure of Charn Thovis—then swooped down and fastened upon the boy, Thar.

They brightened with intent curiosity—and Thar cried out, and lifted his hands to his forehead as if in pain.

"What is it?" Charn Thovis asked. The boy shook his head in bewilderment.

"It's nothing—it's gone now, but for a moment I felt as if someone were digging into my brain and hunting through my *thoughts!*" the boy said dizzily.

Charn Thovis looked back to the gray wizard and saw that now he was bending near the scarlet-clad pirate king and whispering vehemently in his ear. The cool, appraising, thoughtful eyes of Kashtar looked over to where they stood. He asked something of Belshathla, listened closely to the reply, then brushed the gaunt enchanter aside and stood up into the full glare of the morning sun, lifting his baton for attention. Voices died. Stillness came down

121

across the crowded bazaar. Now the baton was pointed directly at Prince Thar.

"That boy," Kashtar said in a clear cold voice. "I buy him for a dozen pieces of gold."

Guards detached themselves from beside Kashtar's bower and came purposefully towards the bewildered Thar.

Charn Thovis felt himself going cold all over. Desperately, his eyes searched the throng and found Barim Redbeard. The burly Redbeard was flushed and angry. He chewed on the ends of his fiery mustachios, but refused to meet the challenging gaze of Charn Thovis.

By his side, Durgan hissed into his ear.

"The cap'n can't do nothing, lad! When the Red Wolf bids for a slave, nobody can oppose him, or they'd end up staked in the sea caves, waiting to drown at high tide, or get eaten alive by the crabs. It's the Law!"

An agony of indecision lanced through Charn Thovis. He could not just stand helplessly and watch the bewildered Thar led away into the slavery of Kashtar. Somehow, the gray wizard must have guessed the truth! Perhaps he *had* read the boy's mind! But what could he do?

Charn Thovis exploded into action. One hand flashed to fat Blay's sash and tore a broad-bladed cutlass from its baldric. He sprang in front of Thar and lifted the sword. Surprised, the pirate guard hesitated for a moment. That moment's pause was his undoing. A backhanded slash with the glittering cutlass sent him reeling back into the path of his fellows in a welter of streaming crimson.

The silence of the bazaar exploded into shouting clamor. Men yelled, cursed, fled from the flashing steel Charn Thovis bore. Another guard sprang before him, raising his blade. The cutlass blocked it in a rasp of steel against steel. Blue sparks hissed as razored edges grated—slid—then Charn Thovis was through his foreman's guard and bright steel quenched its glitter in scarlet gore.

The harsh voice of Kashtar lifted above the uproar.

"Seize the boy! He is the son of Thongor, the prince of Patanga, and worth the ransom of an emperor! Ho—guards! Seize the boy, I say!"

Pikes lifted high, a score of guards came ploughing a path through the throng. Charn Thovis downed another pirate and turned just in time to catch and parry a rapier that darted for his naked back. He beat the rapier away. Cutlasses were not designed for fencing, and his strong wrists ached with weariness. He saw gray-robed Belshathla swoop down upon the boy and snatch him from the slave block in a swirl of neutral-colored robes. Beyond, he saw the line of guards crashing towards him.

Sweat stung his eyes. His breast heaved with every panting breath. It was no use—there were too many of them—and Thar was taken—

He turned, gripped the dripping cutlass in his teeth, and sprang lithely into the air. One hand caught the cross-pole of an awning that stretched over the slave-pens. The other came up beside it. He swung himself up and over it, up the awning to a cornice and then to the rooftop above. Shouts rang out behind him as he raced across the roof, sun-baked stone searing the bare soles of his feet. He came to the edge, peered down for a moment at a narrow alley, then launched himself across the gap to the adjoining rooftop. He just made it, with inches to spare. In moments he was away across the roofs and had lost his pursuers . . . but only for the moment. Soon they would be baying at his heels like a pack of hounds, yelling for his blood.

He was alone in a city filled with outlaws, where the hand of every man was lifted against him.

And the son of Thongor was *taken!*

Huddled in the shadow of a dome, weary lungs sucking in air, he strove to think of a way out of the terrible predicament he was in.

Chapter 18: BLACK CATACOMBS

> Where perils lurk to every side,
> Choose the shortest way.

—*The Scarlet Edda*

All day Charn Thovis hid from pursuit. Abandoning the roofs, he came down in an empty street, pried open a culvert and found welcome, if noisome, refuge in the sewers of Tarakus. As he slunk through the black passages, wading through the slimy murk of foul waters, he blessed the fact that Tarakus' proximity to the sea made a system of underground drainage tunnels feasible. Otherwise, he would perhaps have been hounded down and taken ere now.

Toward afternoon the unbearable stench of the catacombs drove him to the street-level again. The luck of the gods was with him, for he came upon a drunken reveller in an alleyway and soon divested the wine-sodden corsair of his garments, which he donned hastily, having scrubbed away most of the filth from his body. Winding a crimson kerchief about his brows, sliding into the green silk blouse and tight breeches with calf-high boots and crimson sash, he strode boldly forth into the streets. Hurrying mobs of howling pirates swept past him as he traversed the climbing ways of Tarakus. They paid him not the slightest attention. They were scouring the city for a naked, fleeing Turanian slave garbed only in a ragged clout—not for a drunken, swaggering pirate in scarlet and green finery with a dirty face, who roared curses after them as they shoved him aside in the fury of the hunt.

Without being accosted, Charn Thovis in his new guise crossed the city and came to the capacious inn where he and Prince Thar had dined the evening before—the inn where Barim Redbeard and the crew of the *Scimitar* were housed when in port. In all this city of crime he could think of no friends save for them—and he threw himself on their mercy.

They were bewildered and astonished to see the fugitive whom half the city hunted howling through the streets, boldly walk in the front door and hail them by name.

They were even more astonished when Charn Thovis begged Barim Redbeard for aid. He reminded the pirate captain that the debt of blood between them still stood unabsolved. And he acknowledged that the laughing young lad who had won their affection was none other than Prince Thar of Patanga. He called upon Barim Redbeard to remember his native honor . . . for, as Charn Thovis knew, the Redbeard was a son of the bleak Northland steppes from whence Thongor the Mighty had come. Thongor's home was Valkarth to the north of Eobar; Barim Redbeard had come hither many years ago from Belnarth on the shores of Zharanga Tethrabaal the Great North Ocean, an exile fleeing from vengeance, having slain a fellow warrior of his clan in a fit of jealous rage.

"Will not you, a Northlander, stand by the helpless son of your countryman in his great peril?" Charn Thovis demanded, summing up his arguments.

The Redbeard tugged at his fiery mustachios, steel-gray eyes brooding and thoughtful.

"Fry my guts, Charn, I know not what to say," he rumbled. "A Northlander is not withouten honor, even though he be taken to the trade of piracy. And I like the little lad well—I should have guessed there be good Valkarthan blood in him. But I be only the captain here; I cannot speak for all the crew in this . . ."

Fat Blay and lean, one-eyed old Durgan chorused their approval of Charn's plan. The blond giant, Thangmar, for

125

once too serious to grin, raised his great sword solemnly, vowing to help. His mighty comrade, Roegir, the Blue Nomad, uttered a guttural word of agreement, and all the other men chimed in as well, for the stalwart young warrior and the boy prince had won the friendship of the *Scimitar's* crew during the voyage down the gulf to the pirate port.

"Then we're with you, by Shastadion's Green Beard," Barim growled. "But what's to do, lad? We be thirty good men, aye, and well armed to boot, but Tharn—or Thar, as I must call the boy now—be held in Kashtar's fortress on the crest of the cliffs. Thirty men, even be they the crew of the *Scimitar,* have little hope of cutting a red way through all the guards Kashtar will have ringed about his citadel. And the walls be strong and thick, and the gates triply barred with solid iron. If you've a plan in mind, well, speak up, lad—we're with you!"

In swift words, Charn Thovis outlined the scheme that had come to him during the long hours he had cowered in the slime and fetor of the sewers.

It was simplicity itself. Dangerous, yes, to the point of foolhardiness, but still the simplest and most direct method Charn Thovis could think of, to find and free the captive Prince of Patanga.

"The system of sewers that lies beneath your city, emptying into the sea caves," he said tersely. "I presume it lies beneath the citadel of Kashtar as well as the rest of the city?"

"Why, yes." Barim Redbeard looked surprised; then thoughtful. His steel-gray eyes widened. "Do you mean to—?"

Charn Thovis nodded grimly. "I can see no other way to get into the citadel," he said. "We cannot get in the gates—too heavily guarded. Nor over the walls. Hence, we must try the only other route there is—by means of the sewer tunnels."

"But how can we know we are going right, once down in those stinking catacombs?" the Redbeard rumbled inquiringly. "There are no maps, no directional signs. At least, I've never heard of any—nor can I think why there should

126

be. It would be very easy to mistake our way, to become lost, to wander. . . ."

"We must chance that," Charn Thovis said quietly.

Barim Redbeard nodded slowly. "So. Then we had best be about it."

Beneath the pirate city a vast network of black, echoing catacombs stretched in every direction. Foul, oily water gurgled through the winding passageways, or collected in deep cisterns scummed with fetid deposits. Some of the tunnels were so narrow the pirates had to go on all fours through utter darkness. Others widened into huge caverns where three or four men could walk abreast.

They started out with a fairly good sense of direction, knowing their starting point and the way in which the cliff-top fortress lay. They bore blazing torches soaked with oil for illumination, but these were doused as soon as they encountered the narrow tunnels where they must crawl through slush in order to get through.

Rats fled squeaking at their approach. For centuries the red-eyed, shaggy *unza* had ruled these noisome pits unchallenged and undisturbed. Now the furry horde of vermin turned to flee before this astonishing invasion, claws rasping on wet rock, hairless tails slithering through the stinking mud.

Most men would soon have become hopelessly and completely lost in this lightless maze of twisting, weaving caverns. But seamen must develop a sense of direction if they are to survive when darkness floats on the face of the deep and veils the moon and her attendant host of stars. That innate sense of direction served them now as they plodded through the reeking darkness.

They had one sure guide, beyond this seaman's sense. The fortress of Kashtar lay on higher ground than the city proper. Hence, when it came to a choice between two alternate routes, they knew to select the one that rose to higher levels. Thus, with unerring accuracy, they traversed the black catacombs of Tarakus.

They never knew how long the journey took. Doubtless

the pirates took many hours to reach the dungeon pits below the citadel. Here they were cautious, careful to make no sound that might arouse the suspicions of a wary guard.

At length they emerged through a barred grill in the floor. One by one they crept up onto the dungeon level, helping each other out of the vertical pit. Torches flared dimly in the moist gloom. From somewhere in the dark pile of masonry through whose bowels they crept, water dripped endlessly. In the flickering light of torches they examined each other, convulsed in a silent pantomime of laughter. From head to boot heel they were black with mud and filth—a more disreputable band of heroes had never dared their lives to rescue a friend!

With Barim Redbeard and Charn Thovis in the lead, they slunk down the row of cells, keeping to the shadows. No guards were stationed here at the lower levels—doubtless Kashtar reasoned that none were needed, for how could an enemy make entrance from *within?* All fortresses are constructed to prevent an invader from penetrating the walls and gates. No architect had yet conceived of an underground foe breeching the strongwalled defenses through the soft underbelly of the citadel.

They found Thar unharmed, soundly asleep curled in the dirty rushes wherewith the floor of his cell was strewn. He was manacled to a bronze ring in the wall, but the massive hands of Roegir the Nomad and of Thangmar the blond Kodangan giant spread apart the links of his chain as if they were of soft putty. Within moments the boy was set free, and the pirates wasted no time in retracing their steps through the dungeon to the barred grill wherefrom they had emerged from the pits.

It had been almost *too* easy, Charn Thovis was thinking, as he handed Thar down through the opening into the waiting arms of Thangmar below. Somehow he had not really expected his plan to work so smoothly.

Neither he nor any of the others had noticed the dull crystal talisman set in the ceiling above the cell door.

In a distant chamber of the fortress, Belshathla the gray wizard poured over an ancient book of spells, turning the crisp pages of tanned dragonskin parchment with infinite care as he studied the cryptic runes of a lost magical science with avid eyes that alone seemed alive in the dead impassive mask of his emotionless face.

A globe of milky crystal set on a pedestal of black metal flashed with eerie fire like some uncanny signal.

He set the great book down on the marble table and bent to study the flickering crystal. With the palm of his right hand he made a strange gesture over the glassy globe, repeating under his breath a Word of Power. The cloudy crystal cleared, revealing a miniature scene depicted within the globe. He watched as silent, wraithlike, mud-blackened men freed the imprisoned prince. In the dim radiance of the crystal he could not see the features of the men beneath their encrustations of filth, but it did not matter. He was in time to spread the alarm. The magical guardian he had set to watch Prince Thar's cell had alerted him in time to the attempted escape. Within moments the dungeons swarmed with torch-bearing guards who found—nothing!

The captive prince and his unknown friends had vanished as if by sorcery!

The keen eye of Belshathla soon found the key to the riddle. He pointed his staff at muddy stains about the lip of the drainage grill set in a corner of the dungeon floor.

"They have disappeared through the sewers!" the wizard hissed. "Quickly, captain! Take your men down by the same route—I will call out the city guard and have them scour the streets of the city. The dogs must come to the surface somewhere."

It was night when the weary, bedraggled, filthy pirates of the *Scimitar* came out in the street that looked upon the quays of Tarakus. The fresh keen salt breeze from the sea was indescribably delicious to exhausted men who had slithered and crawled and tramped through unspeakable muck for long hours. As the last of their number emerged from the sewer, they stood drinking deep of the clean fresh air, feeling new strength course tingling through cramped and tired limbs.

Just off the further quay the *Scimitar* rode at anchor, her gilded dragon-headed prow catching the faint glimmer of starlight. Another few score yards, and Charn Thovis and Prince Thar would be safely aboard the galley and they could put to sea.

The roar of alarm thrilled about them, shattering the calm of the starry night.

Black alley mouths spewed forth a howling throng of pirates who came pelting across the cobbles toward them. Starlight and torchfire flashed on raised cutlass, dirk and longsword—glittered in the mad glaring eyes of swarthy snarling faces!

In an instant, the Redbeard and his men were surrounded with a swirling mob of vengeful enemies. Steel rang on steel. Boot-leather slipped and scuffled on greasy cobbles. Men died in bubbling groans, as keen blades slashed through their guts—or staggered back from the battle, screeching through the raw red ruin of what had been a face.

Charn Thovis found himself battling for his life! His notched and dented cutlass rang on a lifted *cherm*-shield, which twisted, catching the edge of his blade and snatching the weapon from his grip. A booted foot crashed into his legs from behind, sending him full-length on the cobbles with a grinning pirate leering down at him from above, sword lifted to kill. He knew that in the next instant cold steel would hack into his weary flesh and the great dark of the Abyss would open to receive his spirit.

Then the unexpected intervened.

A tremendous black shadow fell across the sky, blotting out the dim faint stars and hiding the cloud-veiled face of the glimmering moon. Like some vast dragon of the midnight skies, a dark shape glided across the heavens, floating down upon the struggling throng of furious yelling pirates.

The first thing Charn Thovis knew of this was when the ebon shadow swiftly enveloped everything about him, where he lay sprawled on the greasy cobbles, bestraddled by his grinning assailant, who stood with lifted sword ready to slay the fallen warrior.

Startled, the pirate turned a frightened face to the

heavens. Color drained from his features bleaching them to a papery white as he looked forth upon the gliding monster of the skies who hovered above him.

Then a fantastic glare of green-white lightning clove the darkness. Night erupted into searing midday brilliance as spears of thunder-fire splattered about them.

Steel clattered on greasy cobbles from a palsied hand as the pirate who bestrode Charn Thovis let fall his sword.

Death struck, swift-winged, from the skies.

Chapter 19: RACE AGAINST TIME

With triumph nearly in his hand,
The Masked Magician greets the day,
Nor dreams that from a distant land
The heroes speed to block his way . . .

—*Thongor's Saga*, Stave XVIII

All that night the slim silver airboat had drifted on the winds of heaven. For days now, the Patangan craft had tirelessly searched the surface and shores of the gulf for some sign of the missing prince and his companion. They had found nothing.

When Changan Jal and the patrol had returned to the Air Citadel and made their report to the acting Daotar of the Air Guard, the news that Thongor's son had been stolen from the palace by a renegade Black Dragon, the *kojan* Charn Thovis, and that the two had perished somewhere over the gulf, had spread through the City of the Flame, causing shock and fear, grief and alarm. But no one had doubted it—except for those who knew the stalwart young *kojan* from Vozashpa. They steadfastly refused to believe that Charn Thovis was capable of any such act . . . but he *was* missing, the prince *was* gone, and Changan Jal was a trustworthy officer whose word had never been questioned.

The loyalists met in secret and strove to find the reason for Charn Thovis' incredible treachery. Lord Mael stoutly claimed the young officer must have believed Thar to be in danger—that he must have uncovered some sort of plot against Sumia Sarakaja and her son. Shangoth firmly declared that Charn Thovis would never have betrayed his loyalty to the dead Thongor—loyalty that now must be given to the prince his heir. Iothondus agreed, and while the other conspirators argued and debated and puzzled over the bewildering sequence of events, that unlikely duo—the mild young scientist and the fierce Nomad warrior—determined to search out the truth for themselves.

They took a scout craft that Iothondus kept moored to the landing stage on the roof of his house near the Forum of Numidon the evening of the day the news reached Patanga of the demise of the stolen prince. It was their plan to scour the surface and shores of the gulf for some trace of any survivors of the wrecked floater. It seemed hopeless, but Ionthondus could not rest until he had proof positive that Thongor's son no longer lived. And Shangoth felt a strong conviction that the brave, intelligent and resourceful young warrior from Vozashpa would be able to deal with whatever hazards and perils he encountered while shielding young Thar from harm.

The scout craft was swift and powerful, well stocked with provisions, including a tank of drinking water. Its sithurl-powered engines were supercharged and could keep the airboat aloft and under power for many days of flying time. So they set out in secret, determined not to return until every hope had been exhausted.

They found the wreckage of the stolen floater. The steel structure and keel had sunk, of course, but the urlium plating would remain aloft forever until a chance bolt of lightning robbed the magic metal of its antigravitic powers. Of course they found no sign of either Charn Thovis or the boy in the wreckage—not even a scrap of boot-leather or a piece of torn cloak.

They searched on. Iothondus knew, or guessed, that it had been Charn Thovis who had stolen the experimental model of the flying harness from his laboratory. He had decided this from the moment he had learned that it was still a mystery how the young warrior had entered the Palace of a Hundred Kings in the first place, eluding the attention of a regiment of guards. No other solution presented itself to his agile mind but that Charn Thovis had abstracted the skybelt from his unguarded laboratory and used it to fly into the prince's tower room—and out again, with the lad in his arms.

It was this that gave him hope that both might still be alive, despite Changan Jal's testimony that the stolen floater had been torn to fragments by the lizard-hawk thousands of feet above the trackless waters of the gulf. For if they had not been devoured by the sky dragon as Changan Jal believed, they could quite possibly have survived the terrible fall by means of the lifting power of the skybelt.

All day they searched fruitlessly. At night, drifting down to the forested shores of Ptartha, Iothondus moored the flying boat to a tall jannibar tree, and they slept exhaustedly, rising at dawn to continue the hunt. They scanned the beaches along the eastern coast of the gulf, flying low above the wooded hills with signal flags fluttering from the rear deck masts, hoping that Thar or Charn Thovis—if they were about—would see the airboat and know them for friends.

Luck came unexpectedly a day later, when a naval vessel out of Shembis signaled them down and asked for their aid in spotting from the air a pirate ship of Tarakus which had been ravaging the shipping between Zangabal and the Dolphin City. The pirate ship, said the captain, was believed to have paused on its way to Tarakus to take on board a boy and a young warrior who had been found floating in the gulf—or so far-sighted sailors stationed high in the rigging of a pursuit squadron from Zangabal fast on the trail of the pirate craft had reported.

The baffled naval officer did not understand until many

days later why the two men in the Patangan airboat had gone wild with joy at this news, and ascended to streak off to the south without even pausing to say farewell.

High in the night skies above the dreaded City of Pirates, Iothondus let the airboat glide in slow circles as they searched the city below for some sign. The pirates of Tarakus were at war against all flags and nations, so they could hardly land and ask questions as they had in Zangabal and Pelorm. They had no idea what sort of a sign they were looking for, but they scanned the torch-lit streets of the cliff-built city with thoughtful, searching eyes. And at length, as the first faint rays of the false dawn were lighting up the dark east, they saw the sign for which they were waiting.

A battle in the streets near the quays! A howling mob of rough-clothed pirates swept from the black alleyways to attack a small, stealthy band of men—*and a boy*—who seemed to be making their way towards one of the ships moored along the nearer quay. Iothondus gave the controls a sharp turn, and the agile craft slid down through the early morning sky to swoop low over the struggling, cursing mass of fighting men.

He could not recognize either Charn Thovis or Thar through their coating of black muck from the sewer tunnels, but he unleashed the deadly lightning guns with which the airboat was armed, just on the chance that these were the two for whom he had searched. The dazzling bolts of electric fire tore gaping rents through the horde of pirates attacking Charn Thovis, Thar, and the crewmen of the *Scimitar*. The warriors of Tarakus had never seen the terrible sithurl-weapons of Patanga in action before, and they stampeded, half-mad with terror and panic. Within the instant, the battle was over and the airboat dropped down to the level of the docks where an astounded Charn Thovis recognized the familiar faces of the giant Blue Nomad and the quiet young scientist through the crystal windows of the floater's cabin.

With tears of joy in their eyes, Shangoth and Iothondus kissed Prince Thar's hand and clapped Charn Thovis' shoulder in wordless welcome. The young *kojan* hastened to introduce the wide-eyed and mud-smeared pirate band to the two famous courtiers of Patanga.

"We knew you had good reason to carry the prince away," Shangoth growled, when Charn Thovis had told of discovering Sumia Sarkaja in her drugged and somnambulistic state. "I will break that fat pig Dalendus Vool between these two hands when next I lay my eyes upon his ugly face!"

"*Nothlaj*," Iothondus mused, white-faced. "No wonder—now I understand how Dalendus Vool could have persuaded the Princess to become his bride!"

Charn Thovis started. "What? Has the Princess actually wed that greasy *unza*? That must be what they were after, the throne itself—he and that strange companion who goes ever at his side these days, that tall gaunt man in the dark robes, the one with the slitted emerald eyes and his face hidden in the hooded cowl of his robes."

A stab of unutterable foreboding went through Shangoth the Nomad like a spear of ice. His voice was deadly calm as he asked, "A man in dark hooded robes, with his face hidden . . . a man with slant eyes like icy green flame . . . eyes that seem able to numb your brain when you look within them?"

Charn Thovis nodded, wondering at the strange intensity in the tones of the indigo-hued giant of the Jegga warriors. "Aye," he said in surprise. "I glimpsed them when he came up to me in the street that morning, just before you met me near the gates. He was clothed like a beggar then, but I caught a glance at those strange cold eyes——"

He broke off, for Shangoth groaned a curse in a deep, broken cry that seemed wrenched from the roots of his soul. "*He lives!* O Sky-Gods of my people, had I only known!"

"Who are you talking about?" Charn Thovis cried in alarm, shaken at the anguish and grief in Shangoth's ragged cry. The answer came in a thunderous growl that drove cold shock through him and left him gasping.

"Mardanax of Zaar, the Lord of the Black Magicians!"

"Are you . . . sure?"

"Aye! Oh, I know not how that Prince of Darkness

escaped the destruction of his accursed city, but three years ago when I prowled that evil kingdom in disguise, searching for my Lord Thongor whom the black wizards held captive, I saw him well. Aye, I have stood as close to Black Mardanax as I now stand to you, and the memory of those emerald eyes of frozen venom glaring from the shadow of that black cowl still haunts my dreams! Gods of the Sky—I see the whole plot now! It was a bolt of magic struck my Lord Thongor down at the altar—no natural death at all, but the foul vengeance of that City of Evil!"

Iothondus went white to the lips and wrung his slim hands in an agony of remorse. "Ah, where are my wits! I should have guessed it—*nothlaj*, the drug that numbs the will—and black hypnosis, the power of one mind to gain dominance over another! I should have guessed it, when Sumia turned against her dearest friends and withdrew into the seclusion of the palace! And now she will wed with that vile traitor who I doubt not is himself under the power of Mardanax! Aye, the vengeance of Mardanax—to rule behind the throne of Patanga itself!"

Charn Thovis turned to him swiftly.

"Quick. You say 'will wed.' Then she has not actually taken the vows with Dalendus Vool before the altar?"

"Why, no—the herald's proclamation said the morn of the twentieth day of the month of Zamar——"

Charn Thovis turned to the muddy pirates who stood about, gaping at the dazzling turn of events. "I have lost count of time in the rush of events. Quick: what day is this?"

Barim Redbeard rubbed a bewhiskered jowl ruminantly. "Why, *this* is the morning of the twentieth of Zamar."

"What is the *hour* of the ceremony, Iothondus? Think, man!"

The sage stammered, "The . . . ah . . . the n-ninth hour . . ."

"And it must be the sixth or near the seventh hour of day by now," Charn Thovis snapped, mind racing. "We must be away—perhaps, with the help of the gods we can arrive in time!"

Thar grabbed his arm.

136

"But Charn Thovis! What of Durgan, and Blay, and Thangmar, and Captain Barim—we can't just *leave* them here, can we? Now that the King of the Pirates knows they helped me to escape through the catacombs?"

The Redbeard uttered a booming laugh and clapped the boy on the shoulder—a friendly blow that sent the lad staggering. "*Ho!* By the Green Whiskers of Shastadoin the Sealord, never you fear for Barim Redbeard and his men, my lad! Neither Kashtar nor his pet wizard know what hands helped you flee those black dungeons—aye, nor all the men who sought to seize us here, before yonder wizard came out of the skies like a very god to chase them away with his tame lightnings! No, you lads leave, and swiftly, to help Thongor's queen escape the dirty *unza* who would lay their filthy paws on a Northlander's proud mate! Fear not for us—the night was dark, and we've each of us enough foul-smelling black muck on our faces to plant a garden in! Swift now, Charn my lad—be off with you—but don't forget your shipmates of the *Scimitar*. Some day not far off, we'll come cruising into the port o' Patanga to —pay you a visit—mind you warn your fleets and guards that the men of the *Scimitar* be good friends, even if they follow the pirate trade!"

The farewells were hasty but sincerely felt. Before the morning sun had risen free of the dawn mists along the wooded hills to the east, the airboat swung up from the quays of Tarakus with Prince Thar, Shangoth and Charn Thovis aboard, and with Iothondus at the controls the floater circled and rose steeply, angling into the sun, and was off to the north, bound for Patanga.

The scout craft climbed swiftly to the fifteen-thousand-foot level and drove through the crisp air with every erg of speed the young sage could wring from her engines. It was a flight against time—a race against the rising sun—a desperate quest to save the throne of Patanga from the vengeance and the triumph of Mardanax of Zaar. No more perilous quest was ever undertaken for any prize more precious. Though the great Warrior of the West was dead and his soul lost and wandering in the Shining Fields, his heir yet lived, and Charn Thovis and Shangoth of the Jegga would fight to the last drop of blood in their veins before they would permit the traitorous Dalendus Vool to seize the throne of the City of the Flame from its rightful heir, Prince Thar.

Like a glittering arrow the sleek scout clove the skies of ancient Lemuria. Many, many leagues to the north, the bright walls and sky-tall towers of Patanga the Great rose at the head of the Gulf, where the twin rivers of Saan and Ysar mingled their waters with the waves of the main.

Could even the swiftest craft in all the flying fleets of Patanga reach the City of the Flame in time?

Could they raise the people of Patanga to rebellion before the fatal vows were sworn before the Altar of the Nineteen Gods, and the drugged and helpless mate of Thongor found herself doomed as the bride of Dalendus Vool?

Even as the airboat hurtled through the skies of morning, Charn Thovis knew they could not hope to arrive in time.

But they would die trying. . . .

Chapter 20: OUT OF THE SHADOWS!

The Black Magician, at his hour
Of triumph, holds the reins of Doom . . .
Patanga lies within his power
And Thongor sleeps within the tomb . . .

—*Thongor's Saga,* Stave XVIII

The day was come. Morning filled the skies with golden light. The people filled the streets and lined both sides of that mighty avenue, the Thorian Way. Banners flew from every tower and dome and spire. Bright carpets hung from balcony and wall. Bowers of rich blooms were set out and garlands were wound about column and monolith and along the façades of the great arcades. But for all the festive appearance of the city, the people were silent and somber, murmuring among themselves, restless and dispirited.

Before the ninth hour, the wedding procession came forth from the walled parks and gardens that enclosed the Palace of the Hundred Kings. Glittering chariots of precious metal studded and ornamented with rare gems rumbled through the great avenue, drawn by horned and heavy-footed zamphs. In the foremost of these rode Dalendus Vool in sumptuous robes whose wealth of decoration and jewelry could not hide his fat foolish face nor the lust in his weak red eyes.

Sumia rode beside him, magnificent in a gown of gold tissue, strands of glowing pearls woven and braided through her black silken hair. The silent and uncheering crowds that lined the pave were not close enough to see that behind the careful mask of rouge and pigments her face was white and expressionless and her eyes mirrored only emptiness.

Heralds on swift-pacing kroters rode before, sounding the salute of slender trumpets. Rich banners rolled gold and green and scarlet and indigo on the breeze. Other chariots came behind, and among the entourage the aloof and masked figure of Black Mardanax could be seen, though not one of all the thousands who watched him pass with the other nobles of the court knew him for Patanga's greatest enemy.

Down the length of the Thorian Way the splendid procession advanced and into the Great Plaza where a thousand banners rustled in the morning breeze. Forth from the Hierarchal Palace came a procession of robed and mitred priests led by the palanquin of old Eodrym the Hierarch himself.

The two processions merged as they entered the mighty Temple of the Nineteen Gods whose spiked domes clove the fresh morning sky. Into the great hall they filed, to take

139

their places at last before the High Altar where the towering forms of the Gods stood, carven from snowy marble and lucent alabaster. Here at this very spot mere days before, Thongor the King of the West had fallen. He rested there now in a great sarcophagus of sculpted marble that stood below the altar. Sumia's mask-like face did not betray the slightest flicker of emotion as Dalendus Vool led her up the steps of the altar past the tomb of her beloved mate.

The Hierarch met them at the High Altar; the ceremony of marriage began.

A chain of blossoms was looped about Sumia's lax and unresisting wrist; then it was bound about the trembling arm of Dalendus Vool.

The old Hierarch offered them water and wine, bread and meat, grain and fruit.

Guards were stationed at intervals about the tremendous hall. Sunlight streamed through the huge dome of many-colored glass that towered high above the hall. Beams of bright daylight struck gold fire from burnished helm and breastplate and spear.

Chanting began from massed ranks of priests. Father Eodrym asked the ritual questions of Dalendus Vool and of the white-faced young Queen. Her voice was steady, clear and emotionless as she made the traditional responses.

In the curtained box, the peers of the realm sat watching the ceremony. Lord Mael sat glowering and grim-faced, with his two young daughters. Fat, red-faced old Baron Selverus gnawed on the ends of his bristling mustachios, snorting from time to time in contempt of the fat, fumbling bridegroom. Prince Ald Turmis, Lord of Shembis, sat beside Prince Karm Karvus the Lord of Tsargol and Barand Thon the Lord of Thurdis who had come with his son, the Jasark Ramchan Thon. Distress and unease were visible on the faces of these royal guests.

In the shadow of a column to the rear of the box wherein the retinue of Dalendus Vool sat, the tall gaunt dark-robed figure of the Masked Magician smiled a secret smile within the shadow of his cowl. The terrific power of his will was focused on the slim, gold figure of Sumia Sarkaja. Every atom of his magical dominance was exerted upon the slim girl, and he held her will tranced and helpless in the iron control of his own. The moment of the completeness of his triumph was nigh.

The droning voice of the aged Hierarch rose and fell in the ritual statements, admonitions, and queries.

Slowly, the long ritual drew towards its close.

The penultimate rites were nearly ended.

The Hierarch raised one hand to bless the royal couple who knelt before him on jeweled cushions. His mouth opened to utter the words that would seal their union forever—

Then the dome of colored glass far above exploded into a rain of glittering shards as the prow of an airboat shattered through it!

The gaily dressed throng rose shrieking, cowering under the hail of shattered glass. Men shouted and women fainted. Sunlight blazed intolerably through the gaping hole in the huge dome. Guards, struck with falling wreckage, staggered to their knees, dazed, helmetless, spears clattering against the polished pave.

Eodrym paused, mouth open, hand raised, staring upwards in astonishment.

The airboat settled swiftly to the level of the high altar. The mooring cable swung out, the anchor-hook clattering against glistening stone as it looped and clung to one limb of a statue.

From the cabin sprang young Prince Thar, sword in hand, shouting shrilly to his mother.

After the prince, came a grim-faced Charn Thovis and Shangoth the Blue Nomad and Iothondus the Sage.

Charn Thovis lifted his blade and his roaring voice in a great ringing cry that electrified the audience.

"Seize the traitor, Dalendus Vool! Take the robed man in his entourage whose face is hidden! He is Mardanax the Archimage of Zaar, Lord and last of the Black Magicians—and he holds the Sarkaja helpless in his will!"

For a moment a frozen tableau of horror and shock held—then it shattered.

Guards sprang to the curtained box where Mardanax stood. The private bravos of Dalendus Vool sprang to meet them with glittering swords. War-cries and challenges rang out. Steel rang against steel, and men fell in a welter of crimson gore.

Young Thar sprang down from the altar to aid his mother. As he did so, Dalendus Vool rose to his feet, wet mouth working in a frenzy of gibbering rage, spewing blasphemies. One fat white hand clawed at his girdle and tore loose from its scabbard the slim court sword that dangled there. His face distorted in a maniacal spasm of rage, the baron raised his sword to strike at Sumia's bowed head where the coronet of Patanga flashed in ruddy sunlight.

But young Thar struck first! Quicker than thought the boy's small sword blazed in his bronzed fist—to quench its glitter in the fat paunch of Dalendus Vool. The cursing traitor swayed drunkenly. His voice died as his face went flaccid. His sword fell from nerveless fingers to ring like a silver bell against the marble steps. His other hand fumbled feebly with the hilt of the blade that protruded from his belly. He plucked the blade forth and let it fall. Crimson gushed from the wound Thar's strong blow had made.

He fell stone-dead at the foot of Thongor's sepulchre.

Thar knelt and raised his pale-cheeked mother to her feet. Her eyes were wide and bewildered as they stared about at the curious spectacle of battling men and shattered dome and the airboat tethered to one leg of the stone god.

"Mother! Mother!" Thar sobbed, as his strong brown arms went around her lithe waist. "What have they done to you!"

She rubbed her brow and blinked dreamily. The bondage that had held her for so long subservient to the will of the Black Magician had suddenly snapped. She was whole again.

"Nothing," she murmured, caressing the boy's tear-wet cheeks. "I have been dreaming, I think . . . a long and terrible dream . . . but now it has ended, and I am awake again."

Charn Thovis and Shangoth leaped down from the

floater's prow to come to the aid of the embattled guards with their swords. Within moments the last of Dalendus Vool's henchmen were spitted with clean steel. But where was the gaunt figure in the hooded robe? He had vanished from the place where he had stood during the long ceremony.

A cry came from Thar—Sumia shrieked! Charn Thovis and the others turned to see the tall robed figure standing atop the High Altar. How he had come there unseen, none could say. He had melted out of thin air like some ghostly apparition. And now he confronted them all with his carven ebony Rod of Power lifted in one black-gloved hand. Slitted eyes of emerald flame blazed down at them, raging with intolerable fury and hatred.

"Lost! Lost! All—lost!" Mardanax croaked in a hoarse voice raw and choked with madness and despair. His clawlike hands shook from the intensity of his rage. The weird glyphic symbols graven on the Blasting Wand caught and held their eyes.

"All my plans . . . broken . . . come to naught!" the Magician raged, his voice panting and ragged. "But you shall not escape . . . none of you shall escape the vengeance of Mardanax of Zaar!"

Growling wrathfully, Lord Mael took a step forward, gesturing to the loyal guards—but Mardanax halted him, brandishing the wand in a terrible gesture pregnant with peril.

"Stand back, you fools! Power is still mine, yea, power enough to bring every stone of this accursed temple down upon your skulls—power enough to blast the walls of all Patanga flat, to topple her tallest towers and leave this land a black and barren wilderness devoid of life for a thousand years. Do not move a step, any of you, or the black lightnings that slumber in my wand will blast you to gory ruin where you stand!"

The incredible power of the Masked Magician's indomitable will held them frozen with a nameless dread. Such was the superhuman menace in his cold, hissing voice, that not one of the warriors of Patanga dared step forward, although Prince Ald Turmis groaned in anguish:

"The *airboat!* He will seize the airboat—and escape—!"

"Aye, aye," Mardanax panted hoarsely as he clambered up from the altar to the swaying prow of the floater. "All is ... not lost ... if I escape alive ... to bring doom upon you all ... another day!"

They watched, frozen with horror and awe, as the gaunt, hooded figure climbed stiffly to the deck, still menacing them all with the lifted Rod of Power.

Guards strained forward, sweat glistening on their brows, swords wavering. Sangoth uttered a guttural prayer to his primitive gods. Mael cursed sulphurously, face black with effort. But still the unearthly power of the Black Magician held them all at bay.

Then the grating sound of stone against stone.

Startling loud in the tense, straining silence. Eyes rolled in sweating faces, seeking the source of that ominous sound of moving stone.

"*Look!*"

The cry was torn from the lips of Karm Karvus as he flung up one trembling, pointing hand. A thousand eyes followed his stark dramatic gesture.

With a thunderous crash, the stone lid of Thongor's sarcophagus was hurled to the pave where it shattered to a thousand ringing shards of broken marble.

From the tomb, Thongor rose!

His grim, expressionless face was white and colorless as the marble itself.

One great hand clamped over the lip of the coffin. Thews swelled along his brawny arm as the dead king lifted himself to his feet. His eyes were closed, his face cold and dead, as if he slumbered.

They had laid him to eternal rest in the black harness of a warrior, arms crossed upon his deep chest where his hands were clasped over the great cross-hilt of his legended Valkarthan broadsword.

Now he clutched the great sword in one strong hand, as he climbed stiffly from the tomb to stand before their amazed eyes on the steps of the altar where the blood of Dalendus Vool lay in gouts of crimson.

His face flushed with life and animation. The pallor of

death receded. His eyes flickered open—glaring with lionlike wrath—burning upon the ungainly figure of Mardanax at the rail of the airboat.

The magician stood motionless, thunderstruck, like one suddenly bereft of the power of movement. Behind the black visor that masked his features forever from the knowledge of men, his eyes were wide open, green wells of astonishment and unbelieving horror.

Thongor lived once more! His chest rose and fell as he drew air into his lungs. Beneath his bronze hide, his great heart beat with life and vigor. His face was a snarling mask of vengeful fury. Under scowling black brows, his strange gold eyes blazed like twin suns as he held Mardanax transfixed in his gaze.

Against his heart a small idol of green paste lay. A thong of leather secured it about his throat. For three long years had he worn that precious and tremendous amulet which was known as The Grand Negator. Three years ago he had stood thus before another and a darker altar—in Zaar of the Black Magicians, at bay before the triple-headed God of Chaos. Then, in that far land and distant day, his comrade, Shangoth of the Jegga, had struck to free him from the black altars of Zaar. As rays of magic held him frozen in their grip—as the Thing From Beyond hovered above the Valkarthan, to drink his life force and devour his eternal spirit—the sword of Shangoth had struck down Vual the Brain and the hand of Shangoth had snatched up The Grand Negator—hurling it to Thongor where a single touch of that master-talisman had insulated him from the force of magic that beat upon him.

The Grand Negator had saved his life there at the black altars of Zaar. Such was its power, that no force of magic could slay utterly him who wore it. Since that hour, Thongor of Valkarth had worn the green paste talisman against his heart.

And when, many days before, at this same altar, Mardanax in secret had hurled a prodigious blast of murderous magic power against him, the protective charm had shielded his life from the deadly spell. But so intense had been that blast of evil magic that it had driven the astral

145

body of Thongor apart from his physical body, which fell on the instant into a tranced and deathlike state of suspended animation. As the physical body is held to the World of the Living, so the astral form, when it ventures from its envelope of flesh, seeks out the astral plane—that spirit-realm men 'call the Land of Shadows. Wizards and mystics and philosophers of every land and age have studied the science of astral projection—the uncanny discipline by which the astral counterpart of the body voluntarily quits for a time its mansion of clay, to adventure into the Shadowlands.

Thus it was that Thongor entered the Land of Shadows, neither dead nor living, as the ambiguous words of both the Dweller on the Threshold and the God Pnoth hinted at in their speech with him. And thus it came to pass that with the help of Father Gorm the far-wandering astral self of Thongor the Mighty came back from its incredible travels through time and space and between the Planes of Being, to enter again its slumbering body of flesh—*to live again!*

Swift as a striking lion, Thongor's mighty arm flashed back—and hurled the great broadsword glittering through the sunlit silence—to smash into the frozen form of the terror-struck Black Magician.

In the utter stillness of the great temple, the blow was audible—a meaty smack.

The gaunt, dark-robed figure staggered under the impact.

The Blasting Wand fell from clawed fingers, to shatter against the stone steps below. Then, inexplicably, the broken pieces of ancient black wood smoldered—burst into flame. A soundless flash of intolerable brilliance lit the hall, searing the eyes of all. Then the Rod of Power was but dead ash littering the steps.

The wizard swayed at the rail. The broadsword had struck through the robes, keen steel sunk through flesh and bone. The swordhilt protruded hideously from the bony, panting breast like an ungainly fifth limb.

The Black Magician staggered—swayed—fell over the rail to the steps below. He slid and flopped down the steps to the bottom of the stair, and still the great sword ran through his body. But such was the supernatural tenacity and vigor of his life-force that still he was not dead.

He staggered to his knees and crouched, gasping hoarsely. The hood had fallen back, exposing a bony neck and shaven skull whose saffron-colored skin was sallow and tight-stretched, parchment-like over naked bone. Still the black cloth masked his features from view.

With a surge of incredible strength, he clutched at the swordhilt and dragged the length of steel from his body. It came sucking out of his flesh and fell clattering against the glossy stone pave.

Now as he huddled, bent over on all fours like a dying beast, his blood came dribbling out to soil the clean marble. It was thin and vile and black and stinking, like poisonous venom. And when it dribbled over the stone it hissed and smoked and bubbled, eating through the polished marble like acid.

Mardanax fell to one side, his gaunt shaven skull striking against the pave. Even now the dregs of his supernaturally prolonged life were still within his twitching form, but his green eyes were glazed and sightless. One gloved hand clawed and scrabbled futilely against the pave like a crawling spider.

A shudder of revulsion ran through the throng. Under his breath, old Lord Mael groaned. "Aghh—Gorm! Look at *that* . . ."

Before their eyes, the twitching, wriggling half-dead body of the Archmagician was *changing* . . . aging visibly.

Saffron skin wrinkled as a ripple of hideous crawling movement went through it. Suddenly, it was crisscrossed with a net of a thousand wrinkles. Flesh fell from the skull-like head, leaving it bare bone with a thin layer of dried, leathery, parchment skin stretched over it.

Beneath the enveloping robes, the feebly struggling body shrank.

It became hunched and tiny, dwarflike, bent and diminutive as that of an incredibly ancient man.

The next instant a gasp ran through the throng as the

body collapsed into naked bone. Detached from the neck, the bare skull rolled a few feet away and came to a stop, still masked in black silk.

White bone aged, blackened. Fell to dust.

The rotting breath of Time had blown over the corpse of Mardanax and he was but dust. For numberless centuries his magical powers had held Time at bay . . . now Time the Conqueror struck!

Bedraggled, smeared in gore, the dead body of Dalendus Vool lay fallen against the side of the sarcophagus. A huddle of cloth and dead dust, the remains of Mardanax of Zaar stained the midst of the pave. The days of trial and danger were over and past, the adventures and perils were ended.

On the steps, Thongor swept his queen into his arms and kissed her. Then, his arm about her shoulders as her dark head nestled breathlessly against his chest, he put his other arm about his son and crushed the grinning boy in a fatherly embrace, tousled his black mane and kissed him.

From the heights of the altar, where he stood before his gods, the trembling voice of old Eodrym the Hierarch was lifted in thanksgiving.

"*Lords of Heaven and Earth, Father of Gods and Men, we thank thee from the depths of our being that thou hast spared us in our peril and saved us from committing error . . . we thank thee and praise thee that thou hast struck down the traitor and the villian in their hour of triumph . . . and we bless thee that thou hast returned unto us our King, Thongor the Mighty, the Lord of the West of the World . . . .*"

Arms about his beloved mate and his son, Thongor turned to greet his people and receive their homage.

Epilogue

". . . The malice of the Evil City yet lived in Black Mardanax who fled unscathed when shadowy Zaar was whelmed and broken under the thundering waves of Takonda Chann the Unknown Sea. With a bolt of magic he struck Thongor down and sought to usurp his throne, but all his sinister powers availed him naught, and the Gods restored Thongor to the land of the living and bore the gibbering shade of the Black Druid down into the eternal darkness. And all the peoples rejoiced and hailed Thongor the Mighty as Lord of the West, and he was great among men."

> *Or so it is written in the second*
> *chapter of the Fifth Book of*
> *The Lemurian Chronicles . . .*

THE END

APPENDIX

The Source of the Lemurian Mythos

Some readers are willing to judge a story purely on its own intrinsic merits (or lack of merits); others can not rest until they have traced every element in the story back to its original source. They are not content to read of King Arthur or of Robin Hood, until they have probed deeply enough to uncover, in King Arthur, a certain L. Artorius Castus, prefect of the VI Legion, the "Victrix," who was stationed at York during the Third Century and was appointed *dux bellorum* of a punitive expedition against an insurrection in Armorica; and to derive the original Robin Hood from the ancient Saxon name of Merlin—*Rof Bréoht Woden,* or "bright strength of Woden," corrupted and Christianized into the Bandit of Sherwood Forest.

Since 1965, when the first of my Lemurian Books was published, I have been receiving letters from readers all over the world inquiring as to the sources of my Lemurian mythos. Most readers, of course, noticed what is perfectly obvious (and I have never tried to conceal it), *i.e.,* that the style and mood of the books are in tradition of Edgar Rice Burroughs' John Carter of Mars novels, cross-pollinated with Robert E. Howard's splendid saga of Conan the Cimmerian. But they wanted to know where the basic data and framework came from. A few readers, including a university professor or two, asked if I had derived my Lemuria from some obscure corner of Asian mythology. For those among you who are interested in such literary detective work, here is the whole story.

Perhaps the oldest books on Earth are the *Purānas* of ancient India (pronounced Poor-AHN-yahz), a series of partly legendary and partly speculative epics dating from prehistoric tradition. They deal with cosmogony, stories of the gods, the sages, and the heroes, the ancient mythic histories of the Aryan peoples, and of the wars and kingdoms supposed to have existed before formal history began. The term *Purāna* signifies "ancient" and is applied to two great literary compilations. The first of these is called the *Maha-Purānas* (the Greater *Purānas*), and they are essentially religious and philosophical in nature. Authorities say the *Purānas* were first written down in the lost "Aryan" language which is supposed to have predated the evolution of Sanskrit; they were translated into Sanskrit when the original Aryan proto-language was nearly forgotten.

When the scholars and the reference works discuss the *Purānas* at all—which they seldom do, as the later Vedas and Upanishads have almost completely replaced the authority and *cultus* of the Puranic school of lore, even among the Brāhman priests—they are usually thinking of this group, the Maha, which are eighteen in number. These epics, such as the great *Vishnu Purāna* and the *Bhagavata Purāna,* are the ones most widely known, studied and translated in the West. Professor Max Müller in his famous series, *Sacred Books of the East,* translated some of the Maha group.

But there exists as well a subordinate, and more ancient, group called the *Upa-Purānas,* or the Lesser *Purānas,* which are historical and legendary in subject, and almost completely unknown and utterly neglected by western scholars (that mighty repository of human knowledge, the 1959 Edition of the *Encyclopaedia Britannica,* devotes— would you believe, *just one single sentence* to the *Upa-Purānas?*).

So far as I have been able to discover, the complete *Upa-Purānas* have only been translated into English once, in a little-known edition published in 1896 in Bombay, presumably a limited private-press edition, so far as I can tell from the scanty data in my copy. The translation (into English rhymed couplets) is by an Anglican clergyman, the Rev. W. Clinton Hollister, who may have been a missionary. I have been able to find out nothing about him or his academic and scholarly qualifications, but I count myself fortunate to have picked this rare volume out of a bin of miscellaneous second-hand books in New York in 1963. I have never seen another copy.

When I first conceived of writing a Sword and Sorcery novel, I originally considered laying the scene in Atlantis. This notion I discarded for the simple reason that there have been a considerable number of novels about ancient Atlantis—but, to my knowledge, not one single novel laid in ancient Lemuria, which I finally decided to take as my province. I explored the occult literature to see if there was anything there I could use in the way of background data, but I found nothing that seemed suited to my purposes in Col. Churchward. It was a book by W. Scott-Elliot, *The Story of Atlantis and the Lost Lemuria*, that led me to Madame Blavatsky, the founder of the Theosophical movement of the late Nineteenth Century, and to her enormous and fascinating thousand-page work of occult lore, *The Secret Doctrine*.

According to Madame Blavatsky, the human race originated in the lost continent of Lemuria which existed in the South Pacific or the Indian Ocean *before* Atlantis. She was full of Lemurian lore and constantly referred back to the *Purānas*, which reminded me that I had Hollister's book on my shelves, among my scanty collection of Asian literatures.

Anyone willing to read carefully through Madame Blavatsky's cluttered pages filled with weird Buddhist, Tibetan and Sanskrit terminology, will discover that according to her (and to the occult scholars who have come after her, as I discovered through further research), the pre-Sanskrit *Purānas*, which are believed actually to pre-date as oral tradition the settling of the Aryan race in the Indian subcontinent, and to have originated while the Aryan peoples were still a wandering nomadic tribe, relate the histories of both Atlantis and Lemuria. Not under those names, of course, for "Atlantis" is the term used by the Greek philosopher Plato, and "Lemuria" was coined by an English zoologist named Philip L. Sclater with which to label the suppositional prehistoric Indo-Madagascan land-bridge whose existence had been postulated by the Austrian paleontologist Neumayr and the German biologist Haeckel.

According to the occult authorities, where the *Purānas* discuss *Sveta-Dwipa* (the Sacred Land, or the White Island), they are talking about that lost continent or group of islands we know as Atlantis, fragments of whose lost histories were preserved in Diodorus Siculus and Aelian (quoting the historian Theopompos), in the Atlantean fragments of Marcellus, and, of course, in the two famous dialogues of Plato, the *Timaeus* and the *Critias*. And where they mention *Hiranya-Dwipa* (the Golden Land) they are recording some of the lore of that mythic continent we know as Lemuria or Mu.

Further research disclosed the interesting information that almost universally scattered through the Near and the Far East, legend and history and epic contain echoes of these two lost lands. The destruction of Atlantis is described in the Sanskrit tale of *Vaivaswata Manu,* and fragments of what are believed to be the histories of lost Atlantis are contained in the *Saddharma-Pundarika* (available in the H. Kern translation, Oxford, 1909; see Chapter VII in particular).

As for Lemuria, it is believed to have been that mysterious land the Sumerian epics called *Dilmun,* which lay somewhere to the east "where the sun rises." And the great national epic of ancient Persia, the *Shah Namah* or "Book of the Kings" seems to contain memories of the Lost Continent of the Pacific in its references to *Kangha,* the lost eastern island. As well, that cryptic volume of Tibetan myth, the *Bardo Thōdol* (surely, one of the strangest books ever written!) seems to refer to Lemuria in its description of legendary and prehistoric geographies: in particular, in its material on the Eastern Continent known in Tibetan as *Lü-pah,* whose shape is crescentiform and described as 9,000 miles in diameter (see Book II, the *Sidpa Bardo,* for information on the Eastern Continent). I say this with reservations. The symbolism of the Tibetan wisdom writings are all but incomprehensible, at least to western intelligences.

The *Purānas* are very, very difficult to read and almost impossible to make sense out of. They do not even seem to tell a connected story in the proper time-sequence or order of events. I suppose the text has become corrupt during the dozens of centuries the Puranic epics have been told and retold, written down and later edited, translated and copied and recopied by idle monks. As I dug into them I tried to restore the original sequence of the verses into some sort of order. In particular I concentrated on the story of a Divine Hero called *Mahathongoyha*. He first appears (if I have rearranged the verses into the correct order) as a sort of wandering hero of mysterious and probably divine origin. He encounters a great Rishi (sage, saint or wizard, take your pick) named *Sharajsha*; together, summoned by Vishnu, they wage a sacred war or quest against the *Nagarajahs*, the Kings of the Serpent People, whom they destroy with a magic sword given to them by the god Indra. There is also a subplot. *Mahathongoyha* (Thongoyha the Great) rescues the Maharani *Soomaia* from a band of wicked fire-worshipping priests who have usurped her city of *Patangha*; later in the *Purānas,* the hero returns to overthrow these priests and free the Maharani's city by means of the magical *vahan vidya* or Flying Car belonging to Indra, which had been stolen from the god by an ambitious neighboring Maharaj, *Palitahooridya,* who had hoped his court magician could duplicate the flying vehicle with which he planned to launch an aerial army of conquest over all of *Hiranya-Dwipa*.

Mahathongoyha triumphs, weds the Maharani and becomes Maharaj of Patangha; in later portions of the epic cycle he becomes a great conqueror, overthrows the evil princes of five or six other cities, placing several of his warrior comrades in the thrones of these new provinces (such as the young prince of the City by the Sea, *Karamkaravasyu*). He continues to go on quests and missions in service to the wishes of the gods; on one of these he makes friends with the mighty Giant *Sahangota*. Together they overthrow a whole kingdom of black magicians.

With the permission of the god Indra, they realize the

plans of Palitahooridya and create a flying navy of the *vahan vidya*. While adventuring with the friendly Giant Sahangota, the great Thongoyha gains a magical weapon which fires a blinding destructive ray. In the *Vishnu Purāna*, the *Rāmayana* and other works, this weapon is called *Kapilaksha* (the "Eye of Kapila"), or "the Destroying Light." There is a perfectly splendid scene in the *Ashtar Vidya*, in which this mysterious destructive ray is fired from a flying vehicle—it blasts an entire army of 100,000 men and elephants to dust.

Much of the above material can easily be found in one or another form in the later and far better known literary works of Indian writers. The *vahan vidya*, or Flying Car (or Sky Chariot of the god Indra) occurs both in the *Rāmayana* and the *Rigveda*. It also appears in the Persian *Shah Namah* as the Flying Throne of the Shah Kaikooz, and perhaps in the *Arabian Nights*, in Rabbincal and also in Moslem tradition as the flying carpet or King Solomon's flying chair. In the *Saddharma-Pundarika*, the Great Seer Tathâgata defeats the armed host of Mâra with a great navy of these flying vessels. The destructive ray called the *Kapilaksha* reappears in later Vedic myth as the "lightning weapon of Indra" and other gods. To this day the likeness of this hand weapon or prehistoric ray gun can be seen in Tibetan painting and sculpture and *tonka* scrolls as the *dorje*, the curious globular instrument or small heavy sceptre of power carried by certain of the Tibetan saints and deities. There is a scene (duplicated in *Thongor at the End of Time*, Chapter 10) in which the young soldier *Chentovisya*, rescuing one of the sons of Thongoyha (who died earlier in the epic and was wandering in the Paradise of Vishnu, where he would eventually receive a great Revelation and return to *Hiranya-Dwipa* in another incarnation) has a thrilling battle in the clouds with a fierce Garuda Bird which he blasts with the lightnings of Indra via his *Kapilaksha*. The Garuda Bird will be familiar to many of my readers from Indian art and sculpture; in Tibet it is the *Garukha*, a flying Bird-Demon. I have called it the *grakk* or lizard-hawk, and describe it as a species of pterodactyl.

155

As you can see, if you are familiar with the Lemurian Books, I have digested most of these long Sanskrit names into briefer, more easily remembered forms. I presume few save for the occasional Oriental purist among my readers would object too strongly if I cut down *Karamkaravasyu* into "Karm Karvus" or *Palitahooridya* to "Phal Thurid" or turn the friendly Giant *Sahangota* into that mighty Rmoahal warrior of the trackless East, "Shangoth of the Jegga Horde." The *Negas* or Serpent Kings of Indian legend became by an easy translation of ideas, the Dragon Kings, an intelligent race of dinosaurs overthrown by the first men, whose last surviving remnants Thongor and Sharajsha the Wizard of Lemuria slew with the enchanted Sword of Light. As the *Purānas* teem with all manner of fantastic monsters, demons and dragons, etc., I have not found it difficult to turn these into various kinds of dinosaurs and other prehistoric beasts. My zamphs, which I describe in several places as akin to the triceratops, is simply the Indian elephant used throughout the *Purānas* as a beast of burden. I thought it would be a bit of an anachronism to have elephants in the lost continent of Lemuria *circa* 500,000 B.C.

As for the sithurl-weapons, the lightning guns used in this novel and first introduced in the fourth of the Lemurian Books, *Thongor in the City of Magicians,* it was a happy coincidence that while my mythic sources depict a mysterious "Destroying Light" weapon, occultists say the Atlanteans had strange "power crystals" which they used as energy-sources for their vehicles and also adapted as weapons of war. The crystals were called *tuaoi,* according to the Atlantis Readings of Edgar Cayce (you can see them in action if George Pal's enjoyable film *Atlantis the Lost Continent* plays in your town), and I have merely invented the idea that they were *first* discovered and utilized in Lemuria, before being imported into Atlantis.

And then we have the gods. The *Purānas* call them by such names as Vishnu, Indra, Kali, Shiva, and so on. These names I thought far too familiar for fantasy novels, so I simply invented my own. Some of the demons go back to my original source, however; the demon Yamath the Lord of Fire is the Tibetan death-god *Yama*, the Demon King, represented by the Buddhists as a Lord of the Inferno and usually shown wrapped in flames.

One of the Theosophical writers, W. Scott-Elliot, gave me the Rmoahal—the giant Nomad warriors of the Eastern plains. He writes "the Rmoahal race came into existence between four and five million years ago, at which period large portions of the great southern continent of Lemuria still existed." He calls them "a dark race" but I specify their color as indigo-blue, in fond memories of Mr. Burroughs and his green Tharks. Scott-Elliot goes on to say "their height in these early days was about ten or twelve feet—truly a race of giants." In parenthesis, let me call to your attention an amusing sidelight: Fritz Leiber once postulated the theory that Burroughs had borrowed the whole idea of the green Tharks with their towering height and many arms from Blavatsky's *The Secret Doctrine,* or Scott-Elliot. Wouldn't it be amusing if this were so . . . in imitating Burroughs' Tharks, I would then have gone back to the place *he* imitated them from, in order to call them by their proper name—the Rmoahal!

Which reminds me of something else. In creating my Lemuria and in writing its history from the *Purānas,* I have trimmed away enormous amounts of miracles and wonders and religious material (exactly the sort of later, legendary material that accretes around heroes), getting down to a simple story of a wandering warrior who happens to become a great king. In reorganizing the fragmentary and corrupt narrative into a likely sequence of events, wouldn't it be an amusing and ironic trick of fate if I had actually restored what was *originally* the *genuine* history of a *genuine* lost Lemurian civilization into a close retelling of the way things had actually happened! It would be one of the most classic ironies of all time, if in merely attempting to write an entertaining series of fantastic adventure stories, I had uncovered and restored a true lost chapter of Man's past, without ever knowing it.

However, it is most unlikely. Let me add here that I am neither an occultist (Theosophist or any other variety) nor an Oriental scholar. I do not know whether there ever was an actual Lemuria or not. I doubt it. So you will understand that this Appendix is *not* written in order to push onto you, the reader, any private mystical or occult beliefs of my own.

The only thing I *have* tried to do, in the Lemurian Books already written and in those I hope to write in the future, is to create an interesting and colorful world of Sword and Sorcery, and write some exciting novels about it. I have no more noble purpose than to give you what I hope adds up to several hours of entertaining reading.

(Still . . . *wouldn't* it be funny, if I *had* hit accidentally on the truth. . . .)

—LIN CARTER

Hollis, Long Island, New York, 1968.

MORE GREAT SCIENCE FICTION

THOSE GENTLE VOICES
by George Alec Effinger   *(94-017, $1.75)*
What will happen when men from Earth encounter other intelligent forms of life—a race so primitive it hadn't even discovered the spear, or fire . . .

WHEN WORLDS COLLIDE
by Philip Wylie and Edwin Balmer
                                   (89-971, $1.95)
When the extinction of Earth is near, scientists build rocket ships to evacuate a chosen few to a new planet. But the secret leaks out and touches off a savage struggle among the world's most powerful men for the million-to-one chance of survival.

AFTER WORLDS COLLIDE
by Philip Wylie and Edwin Balmer
                                   (89-974, $1.95)
The startling sequel to WHEN WORLDS COLLIDE. Survivors of Earth on Bronson Beta realize they are not the only humans alive—and learn the other group is out to destroy them.

ON WHEELS
by John Jakes   *(89-932, $1.95)*
Automotive revolution has finally overrun human evolution in this vision of the future where to drop below 40 mph means certain death.

THX-1138
by Ben Bova   *(89-711, $1.95)*
Visit the future where love is the ultimate crime. Meet the nameless man who dares to pit himself against the state. STAR WARS director-author George Lucas's original story of man's war for humanity in the 25th century.

GREAT SCIENCE FICTION FROM WARNER...

A CITY IN THE NORTH
by Marta Randall   (94-062, $1.75)

They are set out to discover the secrets of the dead among the ruins — and found, instead, the secret of their survival.

THE BEST OF JUDITH MERRIL
by Judith Merril   (86-058, $1.25)

A collection of the best works of science fiction by the pioneering, feminist, activist author whose stories reflect penetrating studies into the psyche of the women of the future.

THOSE GENTLE VOICES
by George Alec Effinger   (94-017, $1.75)

What will happen when men from Earth encounter other intelligent forms of life — a race so primitive it hadn't even discovered the spear, or fire . . . .